His Lover. His God.

DARRAGHA FOSTER

Author's Note: The love story between Hadrian and Antinous is real. Roman history has shown that the erastes/eromenos relationship often involved much younger males with older males and I, as a twenty-first century author, cannot condone that type of relationship. Thereby, I used creative license to make Antinous older...of legal age in our modern society. May Antinous find my representation of him and his love, worthy.

CONTENTS

PROLOGUE

After I died, but before I rose as a god, the last thing I recall of my life was Hadrian's kiss. His embrace. His loving touch upon my cold, drowned, dead face. I no longer felt pain or anguish. Or fear. When he wrapped me in his arms, two things were apparent. There was no escaping his love. And I never wanted to escape. Here he was, Caesar…king…ruler of the Roman Empire by divine right, and I was nothing but a man born to run wild with bow and spear. Before his kiss, I would have spent my life hunting and fishing. I relished the outdoors and shunned polite society. My mother would have seen me wed. My father would have preferred me become a praetor. I was happier sleeping in a homemade shelter deep in the hills than wearing linen robes or on the arm of a mentor or woman ready to be made wife.

I chose not to be mentored. It was customary. I could learn much as an apprentice, and perhaps even more in *an erastes/eromenos relationship. I did not want to hang on to the arm of an older politician with cold hands and a limp constitution, no matter what he had to offer. Nor did I crave the bed of a woman. When I met Hadrian – all that changed. He was magnificent. Strong. Dark and hairy as a bear. Though he was the most powerful man in the world, the sight of him did not frighten me. He made me hard. He made me desirous of his body inside mine. I wanted to do nothing more than open the flap of fabric covering his manhood and discover what pleasures lay therein.*

Never had I been more overjoyed than when he took me to his bed. I was his cupbearer, and thank all the gods, I became more. I was his constant companion. At night – in the dim glow of the oil lamps in his tent – he took me as if I were his wife. Over and over. He showered me with lavish attention, and from his lips, I drew sweet words of love. There was no embarrassment in him over our relationship. He did not give concern to any who knew of our love.

He ate like his troops and with his troops, and even though he was a true commander and the senate frowned upon his choice to wallow in the mud with his legions, he did. He was one of them. And I was his. Only his.

I will be his – forever. I am his lover. I am his god by his own plea to the heavens upon my death. The great Nile God Osiris listened and heeded the impassioned prayer of the emperor. And I rose into the vault of the universe, a god.

No matter where he goes or how he dies…I will find him. Life is eternal. So shall be our love.

CHAPTER ONE

Modern Era
Cairo, Egypt

Adrian pointed at a beautiful reddish flower blossoming at the edge of mud along the bank of the Nile. "This pinkish lotus is named for Antinous. It has come to represent his everlasting divinity and the love Hadrian bore him." The tour guide stopped and picked the flower. It was the wet season when the banks were flooded. His boot sank. "It is a rare event to have Aquila above us and this lotus in hand. This is the benefit of an evening tour." He looked with a discriminating eye at the handful of tourists in his group. *What do they need to hear? Are they historians or adherents?* He read the crowd. All seven of them. *They are not here for a purely archeological tour. They are here to embrace the love story.* He continued, "Aquila is comprised of the stars in which the Antinous constellation rests. In modern terms, that constellation of the beautiful lover of Caesar no longer exists, but to those who worship Antinous, it is the most important constellation in the heavens."

One of the men in the group spoke up. "He is the gay god. He is remembered. Worshipped. Honored."

The tour guide nodded. "Yes. Antinous lives on. The ruins of Antinoöpolis are proof of that. Unfortunately, Napoleon's army dismantled the city to build a sugar factory around 1789. So much is gone forever. There is a small monument at the place it is said Antinous died. Upper Nile, east bank. Hadrian loved him so dearly the emperor became bereft of heart and soul. I love his history. Not often is a dead mortal deified by a living god — an Emperor of Rome. It's a big deal. Hadrian proclaimed that all worship Antinous, the drowned god. And because of that drowning, which the Egyptians believed was under the auspicious of the god Osiris, he became Osiris-Antinous. If you've not seen the bust, it is in the back of your guidebook. It is regal. Stunning."

"Sounds like you might be a part of that church," another tourist said.

"I am very much in love with the legend." It was a safe answer.

"So much so you do this noisy job, huh? Who knew Cairo and the Nile could be so cacophonic? You might as well give a tour in a subway tunnel."

Adrian, expat, former van-life guy and now with a lucrative Hadrian/Antinous tour nodded at the tourist. "Yes, sir. It is noisy. Egypt is bustling with energy. This site is over four hours by bus from Cairo, and the only thing here to see are pink lotuses under a clear sky bearing the constellation of a god and the remnants of a city built in his honor. It may be noisy, but it has its perks. Now, let's head to the van. We're going back to Cairo, and for those who show up tomorrow, we're going to take in a special celebration. It's October 30th...the day he died. I'll take you to church. Adherents will perform what I refer to as a passion play along the banks of the Nile. The reenactment of his death."

"A lot of pomp for a slave."

Adrian withheld an eye roll. "Antinous was never enslaved. He was Hadrian's companion. He received a higher education in Italy and was afforded the rights of a consort. He was a skilled bowman and helped Hadrian take down a lion in Libya. Hadrian was injured in that hunt. Antinous didn't leave his side and it was his ministrations that helped heal the emperor."

"*Heh.* I bet."

"Homosexuality wasn't an issue in Rome. It wasn't until other influences crept in that it became a sin. Hadrian and Antinous were lovers—but they were more. They were joined. Married. No one called it that, but that's what it was."

"Hadrian had a wife. Sabine."

"Yes, and she stayed in Italy. They never had children. Why do you think that was?"

"He married out of duty—it was the will of the senate—but stayed with Antinous out of love."

"Yes. Hop aboard. We'll see you tomorrow at the church." Adrian tapped his driver on the shoulder to indicate it was time to leave, then took a long look out the window at the Aquila constellation. It always touched him. Always. *Hail, Antinoë.* Antinous seemed like a god he could get behind. *I don't pray, but if I did, it would be to you. The god of awakening, passion, loyalty, and healing.*

* * * *

Far away, in between the raindrops, lost in the mist of time and threads of life, Antinous had been waiting. He had repeatedly refused reincarnation. "I'm not ready," he said firmly. "Until I can be with him, as we were, I shall not return."

"You have been on the books to reincarnate for centuries. You're my only unclosed case. This is the twenty-first century. You died in the first. Things are vastly different now."

"Am I required to reincarnate?"

The timeline service agent sighed. "Yes. It says right here that you are to be returned to Earth."

"By whose command?"

"Which god did you serve in life?"

"I served only Hadrian. And he made me a god. His god."

"Look, Antinous, if you want to stay here, be my guest. I have work to do and will not be able to hold your hand until the next millennia dawns, but let me assure you that you are to be reborn into a loving family. You will have a long life."

The former lover of Hadrian shook his head. "If I am to be reincarnated, then it is into Hadrian's arms and his arms alone."

The agent scrolled through her pad. "That's weird, Antinous. If you are born his child, there would be societal complications. You would never be able to have the kind of relationship you want with him. You'd be his child. Or her child. Or if the person rearing you is gender-fluid, their child. And you wouldn't recall anything, anyway. That's not how it works. To find yourself between his arms, you will need to be in a relationship with him that does not involve blood ties. That is no longer accepted. If you are born—oh…he's already been returned."

Antinous' gossamer form twinkled and rolled. "Send me to him—now."

"It's not that easy."

"Where is he?" Antinous asked with such a demanding tone it shook him to the core.

"Egypt. Isn't this interesting." It wasn't a question. The statement of fact puzzled the guardian. "He is an authority on Hadrian."

"Does he make offerings to Osiris-Antinous?"

The agent shrugged and moved her right hand in a more-or-less motion. "Kind of."

"Tell me."

"He gives tours."

"Tours?"

"Yes. To visitors of Egypt who wish to learn about your relationship with Hadrian and the impact you had on the ancient world. Did you know your bust is in the Vatican?"

"What is the Vatican?"

"It is the seat of Catholicism. One of the major religions that were created after Jesus of Nazareth died and his followers created a church. It is a popular religion. You drowned about a hundred years after the death of Jesus. His church wasn't established yet. Just barely."

"And what of my followers?"

"There are temples in your honor. Several. It seems the Pacific Northwest is very well represented."

"Ah, I continue…"

"Yes. You do, but you could begin again too."

"I will not, unless I am placed with Hadrian, and he recognizes me, and we are one. In any lifetime, I want only him. And I am certain he wants only me."

"Hadrian's reincarnation, this time around, is not aware of his past. He is a good man and follows his heart. He gave up everything and moved to Egypt and runs a very successful tour based on the history and lore of Hadrian and Antinous. He's truly a self-made man. He lived in a van when he arrived in Cairo and now has a company with staff. He's not openly gay, Antinous. He's barely heterosexual. He's asexual—and has been for a long time."

"And he lives in Egypt?"

"Cairo. Yes."

"It matters not that he chooses celibacy. We shall be reunited. Send me there—now."

The agent shook her head. "I already told you it's not that easy. There are conventions to reincarnation that I must follow."

"Who makes your rules? I would speak with this person."

"The rules are set forth by the divine spirits of the universe."

"I am divine. I, heretofore, demand I be returned to my Hadrian without delay."

"It's far better if you grow up in the twenty-first century as opposed to getting dropped, running."

"No time for that. Teach me what I need to know."

"You do not have what it takes to survive in this era. No job. No home. Not even shoes. In this society, shoes make the man. Kind of. You can't just barge in with your dick in your hand and proclaim your love for Hadrian. You will have to court this tour guide. Perhaps help him understand his past life as an emperor of Rome."

"I have never worn shoes. And I know Cairo well. I can sleep anywhere. Any vendor in the souk would consider it an honor to give me shelter."

"You knew Cairo. Its current population is a hundred and one million souls. In your time, it was naught but tribes of humans constituting the former glory of the Ptolemaic families recovering from Trajan's rule."

"Roman rule prevailed. The ancient ones were incest-ridden bastards."

The timeline service agent sighed. *Romans are guilty of incest too. The arrogance of gods.* "You need money. Clothing. A place to live. The ability to speak the language. Latin, Italian, Spanish, and Greek — are changed from your time. English is commonly spoken now but learning modern Arabic would be wise."

"I do not know what English is."

"There's a thing called television. Watch it. Learn the history of the world since you ascended to the heavens as the drowned god. The gay god.

Antinous—it's been nearly two thousand years since your death."

"What is gay? You used it before. It is a word I do not grasp."

"It is a modern term for two men who love each other."

"I am gay."

"Yes, you are."

"I am a god. Would I not be able to assimilate quite readily? Create that which I need?"

"If you return to Earth, you will need to eat and piss and shit just like mortals because your body will be mortal, but yes, I assume you would retain certain divine powers. You've never really tried your hand at godhood. You've been pining away up here for centuries. I'd hazard to guess you'd need plastic as well." The agent paused. "This is new territory. You are divine and will not be born into this era. You will simply appear. There is no precedence for this."

"What is plastic?"

"Credit cards are a form of currency. Plastic is the material from which most credit cards are made. Widely used. It's also a huge pollutant in this era. The Nile delta is awash with waste."

Antinous frowned. "I think you're making this too complicated. I am a god. I can assimilate. Given some forethought, I might be able to help end the desecration of the land you describe. The sacred Nile could be renewed."

Can this man in reincarnation help to end plastic pollution? Interesting. "Perhaps I am overthinking things, but the twenty-first century is not the first. Have you even looked over the edge and stood witness to this era?"

Antinous shook his head. "You will help me?"

"I think I'd better. At least for a little while. Antinous, returning to Earth without being born of a woman into this era is…unique. Counter to the universal plans of life, death, and states of non-substantiality. I'm not sure how this will work out. The constant flow of the cosmos might spit you out. Crush you. Object in ways we cannot imagine."

"I am a god."

"Don't tell people that."

"Osiris raised me on high after Hadrian proclaimed my divinity. Why should this go unsaid? The gods listened to the words of Caesar, and there is no doubt his words still reign supreme."

I do not have the words or patience for this. "The Roman Empire is dust. There are no more Caesars, and Hadrian's legacy — besides you — is that wall he built across Britain. He was an emperor of holding, not expanding. He is remembered for that. You really should not share your divinity in modern Egypt. The Abrahamic faiths are in control. You'd be locked up."

"I know little of those fringe religions. They were not important while I yet lived."

"The cult of Jesus of Nazareth is huge now. You know of him."

Antinous nodded. "Inconsequential."

"Right." *My head is going to explode. Why are gods so obtuse?* "This won't be an easy ride. I can already tell the continuum is going to try to spit you back. Or worse, simply remove you to a ghost realm — that state of non-substantiality. I hope I don't lose my position for this."

"I am a god. Time works for me. I shall appear to Hadrian's reincarnated self and make myself known to him. Subtlety. Romantically."

That might actually work. Huh. "When have you ever used your divine influence? I mean, come on…you've been in the spirit world longer than most."

"Am I being reincarnated in the manner I choose?"

The agent shrugged and nodded. *This is going to be a disaster.*

"*There* is my influence."

* * * *

Antinous had never really peeked beyond the barriers of life and death, as he was completely unconcerned with any reincarnation that did not involve Hadrian. Cairo had changed, indeed. He opened his divine channels to absorb as much of the new world as he could. His journey from un-life to life was not instantaneous. It was literally a traverse across the mountains of death and time and then across the forgetful sea, wherein he began to absorb the modern world. So much had changed. So much had not.

The language was first. Within the confines of language many other things became clear. He ignored the ebbs and flows and ripples of time that pushed against him rather than propel him. It reminded him of a heated hunt in the forest, pushing through branches and leaves, swamps, and streams to get his prey. His discomfort at the crossing was nothing compared to his exhilaration at finally being reunited with his love. The overt newness of everything struck him and enveloped him. He didn't know the purpose for many of the modern items he saw, yet slowly, the new era filled his mind, and he became aware of all he observed. When he saw the pyramids of Giza, he knew he was home.

Antinous had not wept in centuries. Eons. Nearly two millennium. The pyramids were old when he'd last seen them...gleaming white with alabaster casing and manicured bases tended to by adherents of the old ways. The sphinx was now nearly obliterated. *Such disrespect.*

He spoke into the streams of time secretly hoping there would be no reply. He had reached the Nile. Swollen, pregnant with fertility and renewal. Sacred Nile. "I return during the flood, just as when I departed. It is the one thousandth eight hundred and ninety second anniversary of my death and resurrection. So long have I been without my love." *I must show this reincarnation of Hadrian the ties that bind he and I. Make that deeply felt by him. Known by him. And then, we shall be together again.* The currents of time, much like a riptide, pushed against him. A brief fear chilled him as he realized that even he, as a god, could drown in the current. He held himself upright and swam forward. "I am a god. I will make this work. The timeline shan't defecate on me."

CHAPTER TWO

Adrian tossed and turned and tried to get some shuteye in his cozy little flat on the outskirts of Cairo. "I slept better in my van," he scoffed and closed his eyes again…only to see haunting blue ones staring at him with an intensity that made his skin crawl and gut roll. He rose, splashed his face with cool water, and looked in the mirror. The same reflection as in his dream had followed him. He reached for his Trazadone. A sleep aid. Not something he liked to take—but when the ghost of Caesar's lover came out to play, he needed it. "Screw being a closeted medium." He'd always been sensitive to the sights and sounds of the spirit realm. He wasn't alarmed that the ghost of Antinous was very present and literally trying to contact him. He just didn't have the time.

He'd lived through worse. The Hadrian tour

was far tamer than stirring up things in the Valley of the Dead, though Antinous had the only violent death not related to Roman rule in Hadrian's life. Drowned. Then deified. October 30th. Nearly two thousand years had passed. *I'm not going to get any sleep until I address this apparition.*

He aimlessly wandered around his apartment a bit before crawling into bed. "Look…I know who you are. It goes without saying that when one spends as much time as I on the legends and love of Hadrian and Antinous that spirits are awakened. And October 30th is a big anniversary—so the veil is thin. I get it. However, if you have a message for me, get on with it. Otherwise, I need to sleep. I have two tours tomorrow. Be at peace and leave." *Not my first time at the rodeo. Hurry up, spirit. What do you want?* Adrian recognized his personality drew restless shades—but he needed to sleep and wanted to summarily dismiss the spirit. *This one just wants a little attention.* A deep aura of need wafted in with the semi-corporeal memory of what once was. Attention was the greatest gift a mortal could offer. "Fine. I'm not inviting you in, but tell me what you want—in some verbal form if possible—and I'll see if I can help you."

Adrian's return to his soft, comforting sheets became fraught with the anxiety-inducing fact that before him was a full-body apparition. Wearing very traditional Greco-Roman garb with a tight muscular torso, barefoot, and a wild mess of dark blond curls at his head. It was so real he saw the tufts of hair growing on the spirit's toes. He inhaled and was struck by an old fragrance—ancient, charcoaled perfume. Mesmerizing blue eyes beckoned him. The face was instantly recognizable. "They did a good job capturing your true appearance. Those artisans of old." The spirit did nothing, so Adrian continued. "Is there something you need…Antinous?" *I'm too tired to freak out. The veil is thin. I recognize that.*

The spirit's eyes flashed at the use of his name. He slightly raised his arm and held out an open palm. *Just take my hand, sir. Touch me and our journey will begin. That's all I need.*

"I can't give you more than I am. You are my bread and butter, Antinous—but you are long dead, and I am with the living. Perhaps you should seek attention from one of your followers."

Antinous' ghost extended his open hand.

"You want me? All right. Can you tell me what you want?"

Antinous waggled his fingers and thrust his hand forward.

"You want me to take your hand. You want to hold my hand. You want I should touch your ethereal self with my corporeal hand, and then what?" Adrian quickly ran through every horror movie he'd ever seen wherein the victim touched the ghost before exploding or ending up in hell or something. He half expected the walls to bleed and the floor to split to reveal the pit, but as his fingertips touched that of the spirit, there was naught but warmth. Peaceful, satisfying warmth. The spirit didn't pass through him. It melted into him. And there he discovered the nature of the visitation. Before leaving the here-and-now, the words "Oh, fuck" began to pass between his lips but remained trapped. Everything changed. He was no longer Adrian…no longer a tour guide. He was emperor. *Oh, dear God…I am Hadrian.*

CHAPTER THREE

Burly, hairy, swarthy with black eyes that could penetrate a liar and hands that gently tended the lowliest of foot soldier after injury, Hadrian, Spaniard and Emperor of Rome, slid an oil-soaked index finger to and fro into the bum of his lover. His life. The only person on Earth who truly mattered to him in the most intimate of ways. He stretched the sphincter in anticipation of hard intercourse.

Antinous moaned and stroked his own cock. "Please, beloved…please put yourself to me. Tease me not."

Hadrian laughed and aimed his hardness home. The first thrust—always a difficult one, breeched Antinous' anus, sending Antinous' head against the headboard and shaking the foundational tent spikes. The red heavy tent fabric shuddered as Hadrian pounded his lover's ass. Without decorum—or even caring who heard his cry—he uttered low and guttural upon orgasm. He spun Antinous around and greedily sucked his penis until his cock head brimmed and flowed.

Hadrian was large. Broad of shoulder and tall. His body, covered with curly black hair, gave him the overall look of a large animal as it was thick and impressive. He preferred a simple *subligaria* and sandals to robes of state. He was a Caesar for the common man, unafraid to get his hands dirty. Unafraid to be first into battle be it in the field or on the senate floor. In truth, he hated orating and avoided the senate. The senators would tame or mold him into something he was not. He was unyielding. He had been appointed by another rebel—Trajan. Where that Caesar pushed the boundaries of Rome, Hadrian sought only to preserve that which the emperors before him had conquered.

In comparison, Antinous was lithe. Thin but strong. He had not an ounce of body fat. He was all muscle. Rippling, firm, young flesh. His dark blond hair fell in unruly curls, but he kept his beard shorn—whereas Caesar sported a thick, manly one.

They lay in each other's arms, content. Around them darkness had fallen, and the only movement was that of the patrol. The desert could be entirely silent at night. Frighteningly silent. Sometimes the dunes would sing as wind passed through them. A rat would scratch or stray dog howl. Tonight was utterly quiet. Antinous heard Hadrian's beating heart. It gave him intense comfort to know his love lived. The life of Caesar was fraught with peril. From the lion in Libya to the very political structure of Rome—there was always a baneful shadow or enemy bearing a blade.

The elite legionnaires of Hadrian's encampment were ever on-guard. They made sure nothing untoward could come between the emperor and his lover in the night. Or the emperor and his life. Anything—anyone—that tried would be met with a spear to the gut or dagger to throat. Never had there been more loyal soldiers. Hadrian treated them well. Within the heavy regime of duty, they enjoyed status unparalleled to those men who had worn the *galea* before them. Some of the elder generals didn't like it—this equality. They complained even over the amount of food given the legionaries. Too much. Too rich. The old guard believed a little starvation would keep the legions alert. Hadrian disagreed. He had spent time hungry. In his army, no man would ever feel that pain. There were other ways to keep his cohort on their toes than by starving them.

The heat of the Egyptian day had diminished little by night. Antinous rose and then wet a sea sponge with a fragrant blend of water—sacred and rare in the desert—and cooling herbs. The vessel used to hold water in the emperor's tent depicted the Egyptian god Hopi—who represented an abundance of water. The inundation of the Nile. He bathed Hadrian. No one was more trusted than he. So close was he to his love that bribes had been offered to him in exchange for Hadrian's murder. He suffered no fools to threaten his mate and had ordered centurions to publicly and slowly behead the would-be usurpers. With a small, dull blade.

*

Antinous had power. Real power. He sat at Hadrian's side during council meetings. He rode next to Caesar on excursions in the empire. He had helped with the blessing of the wall built to keep the barbarians at bay in the far north of the realm. He had never loved so deeply as he did Hadrian. Every black curly hair. Every scar. Every inch. He lifted Hadrian's right arm and sponged its pit. A powerful manly odor wafted out from the dark recesses and Antinous breathed it deeply. The aroma of his lover after sex was most enticing. Sweat acted as an aphrodisiac. He trailed the sponge along Hadrian's barrel chest and tight belly before dropping to his knees to wash Caesar's cock. He squeezed the sponge over the burgeoning erection, and once clean, he swallowed the member and lavished attention upon it. His act of fellatio was interrupted by a knock on the lintel of the entrance to the tent.

*

"Forgive me, Caesar. I must have a word." The hand that knocked had long planned the action. Counted the hours. Made offerings to the gods for success. The gods didn't care if the boon requested was one of ill intent. It was the attention they craved—and he had sought to give it to them. The Egyptian deities and the Roman, and even those that were worshipped by both peoples. The owner of the hand made his name and intentions known to them all. Marcus Consus of Rome. And he wished to save his beloved empire from what he perceived to be grievous acts. Only Caesar's blood spilled could see Rome renewed. He knocked upon the lintel a second time.

Antinous pulled away and then handed Hadrian a length of cotton fabric. "Wrap yourself and see to needs of that old worry wart."

Hadrian chuckled. "I'd rather have you finish first."

"He won't go away, you know. He will hover about until he breaks words."

Hadrian nodded. "Wise council. Ply those sweet lips with some wine while I listen to my adiutor's most recent words of woe." He straightened his makeshift robe and then opened the heavy tent flap. "Yes, Marcus?" Caesar had a partial erection. It mattered not. Perhaps the head of the serpent would quell the gossip's tongue.

"There is discussion in the camp that I fear you must attend." Marcus, the adiutor—the assistant overseer of the total encampment of approximately a thousand men and hundreds of support staff and camp followers—genuflected before the emperor.

"Yes?"

Marcus studied Caesar's face. His gaze. Nothing but annoyance at being interrupted with his lover was apparent. *That's good. Very good.* "Some of the men who have followers beyond our ranks—there is dissention. The lower ranks. The wives. Even the laundresses and blacksmith gossip."

"Unless said gossip is accompanied by a blade sharper than the tongue wielding it, I have no interest in such things."

Marcus sighed. "The gossip is against Antinous, Caesar. They would see him removed from power. See him removed from your arms and away from influence."

Antinous stood. "That is concerning, for Antinous shall never be parted from me." Hadrian turned and gazed upon his love. "You shall never be removed from my side." He looked back over his broad shoulder at Marcus. "Give me names that I may question the traitors."

Marcus nodded. "Caesar." The eyes and ears of the encampment departed the tent.

"He is a weasel, and it would be better if he had no tongue or eyes in my service." Hadrian pulled Antinous into his arms. "I love you more than water. More than the sky. More than my own life. I love you more than love itself."

"If only I were your wife…at least then I would have the privileges afforded by that office."

"You are my wife in practice if not by law. Perhaps I should seal your fate to mine in such a way that no one will question your authority. I shall make you my heir."

Antinous startled. Hadrian drew him in tighter. "Caesar, would not a child of your body be better suited as your heir? A child of your body could be named the next emperor of Rome."

"I am not Trajan's child and yet I am emperor. I shall never have children with Vibia Sabina. Our marriage has never been consummated. She has taken lovers with my blessing but is careful not to bring a child into our house in Rome. It is my right as emperor to name an heir. My predecessors adopted. So shall I."

"I am blessed by you, Caesar, but I wonder if perhaps you should sire a child by another noble woman—a blood relative—as is Vibia, and name that child as heir. Surely you will bring sons into this world. Strong sons."

"Antinous, my love—I have tried to take women to my bed but I find the marital act or even that same action with a concubine unpleasant. I do not become aroused. I am not desirous of the parts of a woman most men clamor for. Breasts are for feeding children and the hidden parts between their legs are for birthing them. The taut body of a man, I find remarkably appealing. That as it may be, I want only you. I want only you for the rest of my life, and should the gods bless us thusly, for all eternity."

Antinous rested his head against Hadrian's chest. "Yes, Caesar. I am honored to be your lover and heir." *I am no Caesar. I could never rule an empire.*

"You are my life."

"Which, perhaps, is why the camp followers are frustrated. You have not walked among them or chosen a whore with whom to lay. You have your body servant gather your wash and you tend to cook your own food. That man Marcus is not your ally. And he looks at me as though I am a piece of honeyed fruit."

"If it is my hand that prepares the food, I am assured it is to my liking and is not ever to be poisoned. And as for Marcus...I will not fault him for finding the sight of you delicious and tantalizing."

"Perhaps if you behaved a little more like your predecessors and whored and gave commands of the wash women and complained at the blacksmith…the words against me would end."

"I could pay a woman to come to my tent and clean it. I doubt giving such a command to my body servant would appease the masses."

"Yes. Said woman could then spread rumors of your prowess and strength upon her as you savagely took her over and over. Your servant is mute, Hadrian. That would never do."

Hadrian laughed. "Indeed. And do you believe that a cleaning woman will quell any nonsense about you?"

"My father taught me to keep my friends close and enemies closer."

"A wise man who raised a brilliant son. And now, let me demonstrate upon your body what the cleaning woman shall gossip in passionate form."

Antinous never refused Hadrian. Never. How could one refuse the affections of a god? The divine emperor. It didn't matter if he was tired or hungry or just not interested in sex. Hadrian's needs always came first. Hadrian had never forced him, abused him, or in any way made him feel lesser than any Roman—even though he was Greek by birth.

Hadrian's word was law. All acted directly upon any command. The *Cohors Prima Centuriae* of about eight hundred men, plus auxiliary—the *Supernumeralii* soldiers and camp followers from *medicus* to whore—all bowed to Hadrian's will. He was Caesar and ruled with absolute power. Hadrian loved him so dearly that should he ever ask not to be used—not to be made love to— Hadrian would agree. *I'm not a slave. I'm his lover.*

His wife. I wish I could bear him children. He lurched forward with Hadrian's powerful thrusts and gripped the pillows as he was filled to the brink and hot sperm, having no room to settle, trickled out of him. Hadrian's sacred seed.

He was hard. Though he was tired, his body responded to Hadrian's reach around and he, too, achieved orgasm. Sated, he rolled away and then covered himself with an Egyptian cotton blanket heavily embroidered with images of the gods.

"Sleep, my love. Morning comes soon enough."

Antinous had expected to feel Hadrian's large body beside him as sleep overtook him, but it was not to be. Hadrian dressed only in his *subligaria* before leaving the tent.

CHAPTER FOUR

Hadrian cut an impressive swath of a man, even only garbed in his loincloth. Dark skin, black curly hair of head and chest. Penetrating brown eyes. That was the Spaniard in him. The aura of power came from the gods. He didn't suffer fools—and Marcus was a fool. A thousand tongues could speak ill of Antinous or raise threats—and all of them would be unfounded. Except Marcus. *He's a jealous man. His passions runs to dark places that most dare never tread.* "I know you are lurking about. Show yourself and speak to me of the dissenters in the masses," Hadrian said into the night air. The legionnaires guarding his tent did not reply, but Marcus did. Hadrian thought his voice more serpent than human.

The weaselly assistant bowed. "Caesar."

"Speak."

"Alas, Caesar, their names are not known to me. Perhaps if we stroll through the camp, I can point them out to you."

"Attend me," he said to one of the sentries at his tent.

"Without the guard, perhaps. Sir. If you are less formidable…"

Hadrian stopped Marcus. "I will not go into the camp-follower city without a guard—especially when I am only dressed in a loin cloth and sandals." *Does he think me a fool? Does he wish to thrust a blade into my belly? No guard? Surely, he jests.*

"Perhaps Caesar should don his *toga picta*," Marcus said softly.

"It's too hot. Come now. Let's away to the supporters' encampment. The hour is late, and I am tired, but I would not see Antinous' name belittled." *Your name, however, I shall trample underfoot if this is as I suspect. A poor attempt at an assassination. Who pays you, Marcus? That's who I want.* "Have you a sponsor in Rome, Marcus? A rich senator who sees to your comforts over and above the pay you receive as assistant overseer?"

"From time to time I receive a stipend from a group of politicians, though it is not much and there is no praise heaped upon me by their orations."

"Who?"

"I received a small sum and some trinkets from Longinus Marcellus a few moons ago. Before we settled here by the Nile."

"When his rider brought me news from the senate?"

"Yes."

"What is Longinus' plan? Does he wish you to curry favor and become chief overseer so he may fill the ranks with his men?"

"I suspect so, Caesar."

Marcus led the way through the sleeping soldiers and sentries and into the throng of camp followers. The followers' camp never slept. From whores to hunters, activities of daily life continued. The bakers were awake. Kneading and shaping dough made from good Egyptian grain and Italian oil to be baked in ovens built with stone and mud atop donkey-pulled carts. A thousand loaves baked, ofttimes twice daily. Already hundreds of loaves had been prepared and put to cart and delivered to the legions for their morning meal. The bakers kept a tally, using chalk and slate with notations as to what quadrant of the camp each cartload was headed. Their grain stores were heavily guarded by Egyptian conscripts and preserved in their fashion. Hundreds upon hundreds of large earthenware jars were buried in mud brick storehouses not too far from the camp, but far enough away to avoid the inundation's reach. It was said the sand surrounding the grain bins smelled of flat bread due to the ambient heat. Hadrian had never taken the time to explore the area. He had given orders that the wheat be kept safe and had never again troubled himself with the matter. His word was law. His orders, divine.

One woman, old, hunched over, and nearly toothless stood and greeted Hadrian. "Hail Caesar. What brings you to the supporters' camp at this hour? Can I get you a hot loaf?"

"Thank you, no. Every loaf should go to my

soldiers. I have simple tastes. Porridge and wine are my staples. *Posca* keeps me humble." He laughed at his own joke. "I drink with my men, but the good breads and other foodstuffs, I leave for them." Hadrian paused. "Does this bother you?" He side-eyed Marcus with contempt and disdain. *I swear Marcus makes mental notes of my generosity to my men so he may relate the information to villainous ears in Rome. I see him trying so hard to keep calm. Beads of sweat on his brow tell a different tale.* Hadrian watched the baker—who was obviously desirous to break words but was holding back. "It's not a trick question, woman."

"I'm sorry, Caesar. I'm not often queried about my preferences by the likes of…well…*you.* Simply stated, I have no concerns over how you feed your troops. I am paid. I am given grain untainted by rat feces or mold. I follow the armies with my oven and have since the days of your predecessors. I am a baker. This is what I do. The concerns of state are not my affair."

Hadrian glanced at the small shrunken form of Marcus. "Well, the woman who provides the bread has no issues with me or Antinous."

The baker chimed in. "Antinous is a polite young man. He serves you well as your cupbearer, Caesar."

Hadrian chuckled. "So he does. Indeed." He glanced at his centurion guard. "Have you a copper?"

The guard nodded.

"Give it to the baker. I will see you reimbursed."

The guard reached inside his belt and then pulled away with a copper coin. He tossed it to the baker. "Caesar."

"Thank you." The woman held the coin up and bowed her head to Hadrian.

"Tell me, woman, have you heard of anyone speaking ill of Antinous or myself? I come not to punish but to clarify, so have no fear in sharing names with me."

A small crowd had gathered. The laundress, the armorer. Two young whores. Brother and sister by the looks of them. The son of the blacksmith and the hunters, no doubt setting off to kill fresh meat. An ibex, perhaps. Or gazelle. Anything but camel. If a wild camel was caught, it was trained, not eaten.

"Truthfully, Caesar..." The woman glanced at Marcus, then at the small crowd. "Only your aid speaks ill of you and yours."

Marcus protested. "Why, you old bat! How dare you!"

"I sleep little that the bread is ready for the troops when dawn breaks. I hear whispers. And I've seen you prowling about like a rat on a moldy crust."

"As I suspected. Thank you." Hadrian reached out quickly and took Marcus by the tunic neckline. "Your dagger, centurion."

The guard passed Caesar his blade.

Marcus squirmed. "No. I have done nothing."

Hadrian squeezed the fabric tightly. "Why tell me no when you, yourself, have brought upon my judgement by speaking falsely against Antinous?"

"I did not mean..."

"You did not mean what? To interrupt me with fables and lies? I am a busy man, Marcus." He cut away the blue cloak hanging regally off the liar's shoulders. "You are hereby demoted to baker's apprentice—and even that noble task is above you. I will not see your face again." He turned to the baker woman. "And you, my fine woman, shall receive three coppers a week for training this outcast in the fine art of bread. His life shall be bread. His nights shall be bread."

"Yes, Caesar." The woman stood tall as the centurion placed Marcus into her care. "The ovens need new clay. I'll teach you that first."

Marcus protested. "I am a nobleman and second only to your council of generals."

Hadrian laughed. "No longer."

*

Marcus went rigid as his world began to collapse. *It has all been planned. How can things be going wrong when the plan is perfect? This cannot be.. I am to be elevated by his death, not put to manual labor with the working dregs of society. If I fail now, the senate will have me murdered in my sleep. My mistress will be raped and torn to pieces. My possessions distributed or burned. I must stop Hadrian from further dalliance with that Greek lad and force his attentions to Rome.* In a furious rage, he put hand to dagger, and his jealousy seeping from him like an open wound, he forcefully lunged at Caesar. He had a knife—his own short knife often used for meals. He stabbed Hadrian's ribcage. The emperor gasped and he and Marcus locked gazes as the blade passed through flesh and bone.

The baker lunged at the attacker and threw

herself atop him, though it was clear the dagger had ripped into Hadrian's side. She spread her weight atop Marcus and pummeled his head with her fists. The knife, she knocked from his hand. "Shall I strangle him for you, Caesar? These hands are strong in your service."

"I do not wish the hands that bake bread to be stained by such things. Guard…"

The guard glanced at Hadrian. "Shall I dispatch him?"

Hadrian nodded.

The guard gently bid the woman to move, and he lifted Marcus by the shoulder of his tunic. In one swift move, he broke the neck of the former assistant overseer. The soldier looked at Hadrian. "Too good of a death for an assassin. Better he died slow along the Nile in crucifixion."

Though injured and bleeding, Hadrian lifted the baker to her feet. "You are an honorable woman. Your loyalty shall be rewarded. Whatever property this man had, is now yours. From his tent to his horse to his personal stores." *This is a deep wound. I must remain calm. Dignified. I cannot allow this attack to reveal any weakness in me.*

*

The guard side-eyed the lifeless body of Marcus. It was his job to protect Caesar. He was a bit desensitized to death—and he knew it. "Apologies for not stopping him, Caesar. The little weasel was clever, I'll give him that. I shall escort you to the *medicus*."

"He stabbed me. He stabbed a living god." Hadrian pulled away his hand covered in blood. "To attack me is to attack the gods. What gall."

The baker stepped forward. "May I, Caesar?" She gently reached out and placed sticky dough over the deep, jagged wound. It essentially sealed the gash. "Leave it there until you can be sewn by the *medicus*. If he isn't drunk, he should well be able to hold a needle and thread and perhaps even wash his hands first. Do I still get the money?"

"Ingenious. The blood flow is completely staunched. And yes, I'll see to your payment, though you are now without an apprentice. All that was his is now yours."

"I have many hands eager to learn my skills. Bread is the staff of life—even lifesaving. Go now, Caesar. I fear for you." Treating Hadrian as if he were her son, she passed him off to the guard. "Take him to get stitched. I'll watch over the corpse. Thank you for honoring the promise of three coppers, though this sad little man will no longer learn how to bake. Will your scribe bring me a letter of claim that I may collect his belongings?"

"Yes, but go now and collect anything of value before vultures descend. My guards will see that the jackals break their fast well this day." Hadrian allowed the guard to support him as they walked. Another legionnaire ran up. He assisted their emperor to the medical tent.

"Hail, Caesar," the woman replied. She pulled on the sleeve of her fellow baker, and carrying empty baskets, they ran off to find the tent of the late assistant overseer.

Hadrian ambling through the camp followers

always gave onlookers pause. At this very early hour of pre-dawn, with blood covering his hands and side, and being escorted bodily by legionnaires, even more so. Some had never seen him up close. The rumors of his great stature and glory were true. Clearly true to those now standing agog.

The *medicus* had more scars than a legion of men. His long hair fell into greasy curls at his shoulders, and his tunic had bloodstains. "Caesar." He genuflected briefly. "Stabbed, were you?"

"Yes."

"Ah, your wound has been sealed neatly, but dough once applied can be tricky to remove without pulling the wound further. It is an old battlefield trick, and one I've seen used often. Biting ants can close a wound too. Though we are far from a jungle region where one might find them. Caesar, lay down on your left side that I may tend to this gash on your right."

Hadrian complied. "In all my years, I have never seen dough used as a poultice. Ingenious. I owe the baker my life."

The *medicus* carefully lifted the drying poultice of dough. Blood immediately oozed. He did not hesitate to wipe away any residue and stab the gash with a needle and thread.

Hadrian wasn't going to allow himself the privilege of crying out, though the pain was intense. Always strong. Always composed. Except in the arms of Antinous—when he could truly be free. "Is it deep?"

The *medicus* didn't pause his needlecraft to reply. "Fairly. And jagged. And in a place that makes healing tricky. Looks like a *puglio* mark."

"Yes. It was. No doubt infected with the ailments of whatever sores that bastard had in his mouth. Thank you for taking care of this," Hadrian replied. *And man…bathe. The Nile is but a short distance from us.* He didn't want to insult the physician by choking on the man's body odor.

"Seventeen stitches to close it. Please keep it covered and dry for a week. If infection sets in, send for me. I will reassess soon. You can wash it with *posca* and keep honey under the linen to avoid infection. I do hope the person who did this to you has been punished."

"His body lies cold."

"I see. This man was known to you."

"Yes. A trusted member of my council."

"No longer." The *medicus* wrapped a clean linen bandage soaked in honey over the wound and then secured it with another strip of fabric. "The honey prevents infection. It is a sweet blessing from the gods."

Antinous burst into the tent of the *medicus*. "Caesar! Thank all the gods you live. I was told of the attack and feared the worst."

Hadrian stood slowly. He withheld a wince as the stitches pulled. "Nothing short of death will keep me from your side and even death could not hold me. This little scratch is nothing."

"I don't know if I should slaughter a goat to thank the gods or just weep at your feet."

"The gods don't need another goat, and I would rather hear laughter from your lips than see tears fall from your eyes. Go back to our tent, Antinous. I have matters to which I must attend. Such as appointing another assistant overseer. It seems my trust may have been misplaced in Marcus."

"He served you for years without incident."

"He wished me harm. I must devise his loyalties and quash them. I took note of his new sandals—Egyptian, quality handmade. Finest leather. His tent has some new embellishments. He's been paid off."

"I would sharpen my dagger on the throats of any in collusion."

Antinous and Hadrian shared a thoughtful moment. Hadrian sighed. "I would not see your hands bloodied."

"I would kill for you. I would die for you."

"Let's hope these things do not come to pass." Their hands briefly clasped. If the gods celebrated love, then their revelry never died when toasting the love of Hadrian and Antinous.

Hadrian broke from his gaze into Antinous'. "Centurion, see Antinous safely to our tent and double the guards. Rouse the *aeneator* to summon my most experienced legionnaires. I want the *decanus* to meet me in the clearing. Full dress. Pikes, swords, and shields. Awaken the generals."

The centurion pounded fist to chest and then motioned for Antinous to follow him.

"I will fight for you, Caesar," Antinous said as he stepped from the *medicus'* tent.

"I know. If it comes to that, I will give you my sword to wield against my enemies." Hadrian called after to the centurion. "Have my dresser bring my armor and *posca*. The torch bearers should set up along the parameter. We have hours until dawn but this cannot wait."

"Yes, Caesar."

Hadrian sat, reeling. He ran over the events leading to the present moment. His actions. His orders. *I have called out a formation, in the wee hours of the morning, because one man threatened me. One man. I have been hard pressed by other assailants and won.* He touched a scar across his belly. *I won. I shall win again. That little weasel used Antinous against me. I will not stand for that. Antinous is the earth upon which I rule and the heavens which are my divine right. No. I shall not see his name sullied.*

"Opium, Caesar? The pain will be significant once the adrenaline wears off." The *medicus* motioned to a collection of small vials in a box.

Hadrian shook his head. "I'd rather not until the need calls for it."

A legionnaire — a very young man of not more than sixteen years, fresh faced with a uniform too large — appeared at the entrance of the medical tent. "Caesar."

"Yes?"

"Your overseer, Caesar…he was found dead but moments ago. His throat and his…"

"Go on. If you wish to be a true man of the republic, you must be able to orate well in times of peril."

"His throat was cut and his member, Caesar…it had been sliced off and placed inside the gash."

"Well, that's one way to rid yourself of a problem. Have the body bound in linen and given to the *dissignatore*. He honored the gods of Rome — so I will bury him thusly. I will be along presently."

The youth pounded his fist against his breastplate. "Caesar." He turned before he hurried away.

"It appears you are in need of an overseer and an assistant now, my liege." The *medicus* fussed with the bandage across Hadrian's torso.

"There are many who seek to increase their status. I need only reach out and ten men will rally to the positions. I will not choose from among them. I seek only a man of humility. A man who stays in the shadows yet knows all."

"You seek a sorcerer."

"I may. Yes."

"Can I escort you to the clearing where your troops gather?"

"Stay close, physician."

"As you wish, Caesar."

CHAPTER FIVE

Dressed in a tunic and robes of state, his wound painful, yet bound tightly to prevent seepage, Hadrian forced his way into the center of the small but elite gathering of his troops. "An attack on me is an attack on the empire. Tonight, words were levied against Antinous by a once-trusted man, and when I investigated the matter, I was cut. His body is now outside our fires in the high desert where jackals may feed upon it."

A harried woman with hennaed hair and gaudy rouge—a whore—appeared from the shadows. "May I speak, Caesar? And though my words might be my last, they must be said."

"You are his woman?"

She nodded. "And now without a home since the baker took all that Marcus had."

"Do you seek compensation for his death?"

"No. I want nothing from you, except to break words."

"Explain yourself." Hadrian's command echoed through the enclave.

"Marcus was sorely aggrieved by your practices. Since I am to die this night as I stood in his confidence, then I shall speak on his behalf. You spend more energy with your consort than you do with your troops. You do not love Rome. You love him. Marcus wanted only what was best for the legions. A leader who stands first for Rome."

"I do love him. As deeply and completely as I love Rome. It is my right to have a lover—or a hundred if I wish."

The woman continued, "I believe you do the empire a great disservice by spending your seed upon the backside of a male rather than by siring heirs. Your duty as emperor is overlooked."

"I am Caesar and the choices I make are for Rome."

"It would be better if your wife ushered forth your heir."

"You speak boldly," Hadrian replied.

"The dead have no worry of repercussion."

"Then I grant you death." He looked to the commander of his host. "Crucify her." Hadrian winced. "My generals, you are to root out dissenters in the legions and within the camp followers. Bring them to me. I want you even unto the streets of Al-Minya and Cairo if necessary." He beckoned to his chief tribunal. "Dismiss them. I have a mission for you."

The *Tribunus militum* called to the cream of Hadrian's Egyptian army, "Legions, you have your orders!"

The soldiers neatly broke formation presumably to begin the process of execution and questioning the thousand souls in the camp and beyond.

"Tribunal, after she is crucified, please seek to end her life quickly. I would not have her suffering prolonged. Understood? And while the hammer rings, press her for the name the man whose payroll Marcus was upon." Hadrian paused. "Now…I must retire. The wound is painful. Please escort me to my tent."

CHAPTER SIX

"I've never known you to so abruptly order an execution," Antinous said as he helped Hadrian from his robes and armor. "Gods, Hadrian...you didn't need to don full regalia tonight. Your wound is weeping from the pressure."

"Oh, dearest Antinous, I love your innocence. I would reply with a question to you. Have you ever known there to be an attack on my life?"

"No. Other than the lion in Libya, no."

"Then it is my duty as emperor to make an example of Marcus and his treasonous bitch. She wanted to die. She all but begged me to kill her. Had Marcus not been summarily dispatched by my guard, I'd have crucified him too." Hadrian paused. "His mistress would have found no quarter in the camp followers and her life would have been lived as a diseased whore, being passed from man to man of meager means. She may have even walked into the Nile and drowned herself."

"Osiris would accept her should she end her life thusly. He is a just god."

"He can claim her from the pyre."

"Will you watch?"

"The crucifixion? I should, but I whispered to my commander to have her die quickly. And quite frankly, I do not enjoy the spectacle of execution. It is a necessary evil."

"Her legs will be broken, and her body pierced. It is a sorrowful way to die."

Hadrian reached out for Antinous. "There are worse ways, beloved. Now, I must rest. I thought I would not need an elixir, but I was mistaken. Have the physician bring me Egyptian opium mixed with vinegar and honey. A small portion. I would like to relieve the pain but not sleep for three days. He's probably drunk in his tent as he wandered away from me toward the Nile — or perhaps the *posca* tent — before I broke the gathering."

"Yes, Hadrian."

Antinous stepped away from his lover and bade one of the centurions to fetch the physician's good medicine. He sat outside the tent, next to small fire and drank a *posca*. *If Hadrian had died…I would have been next. And my death would not have been swift. Surely, I would have been emasculated for not being born a Roman citizen, but a son of a Greek merchant and all that entails. Emasculated. Disemboweled. Beheaded. Thrown to the jackals. I believe in the gods of this land more so than those of my father's. May they watch my back. So many gaze upon me as though I need pity or rescue. I am not Hadrian's slave or servant. I am his everything. He is mine.* He looked at the clay cup in his hands. *It was a cup that brought us together. A simple cup.*

CHAPTER SEVEN

Summer in Bythinia. Hot. Dry. As dry as the desert expanse before him now. The weather may have had something to do with Antinous' father offering his son as cup bearer to the emperor years prior. Always the merchant. His son was certainly a commodity worth trading. Antinous had the skill and manners to serve Caesar, but his temperament was far too wild. He wanted only to run in the hills and hunt or fish. He would not disobey his father, though he was a man and able to make a man's decisions. He didn't balk when he was told he would stay with the emperor as a body servant during the time Caesar was in Bythinia. He went willingly.

Antinous chuckled and turned the empty cup in his hands. The fire was too hot, and he moved his stool back. In the east, the sun rose. The seasons had changed several times since he'd first offered

Hadrian a cup and felt the stimulating and intoxicating touch of Caesar's fingertips. That very night Hadrian took the *posca* from Antinous' hands and then took him.

"You can refuse me, Antinous. I will not take you against your will. You are not my slave."

"Do you mean to make love to me, Caesar?" *I want it. I want him in me. I want him more than I've ever wanted a woman. This man…this large, beautiful man. I must have him.*

"I do."

"I am yours to command, Caesar."

"I don't want to command you. I want you to want this."

Antinous lowered his gaze and whispered softly as he traced the outline of Hadrian's erection through the fabric of the emperor's *subligaria*, "I want this."

Hadrian lifted Antinous' chin and leaned in for a kiss.

That kiss never ended.

From that day forward, Antinous was favorite of the emperor. His constant companion and lover. As a part of Hadrian's retinue, he saw the world. Hadrian traveled all roads within his empire and with him, his legions and romantic partner. He marveled at the great, long wall constructed in the far north and the pyramids of Giza. He had been educated in Italy but had never seen the country through the eyes of love. *There is no greater love than ours. I am the most fortunate man in all the world, for I am companion to the divine emperor. With a target on my back. A moving target since at his side I have seen the world. The glory of Hadrian's Rome.* Antinous slightly bowed his head. *Osiris, hear my prayer and protect Hadrian from harm. As you bring flood waters and make the plain fertile and as you protect those who walk the path to the underworld, protect him. I will make an offering to you in return. Send me a sign in agreement, and it shall be done.* He'd never really prayed before. Not from the heart. Not for anything or any cause. To call upon a god was to be noticed by them and being noticed by them could bring salvation or pain. *Hadrian's life means more to me than my own. For him, I accept whatever it is you wish, great Osiris, from me or the work of my hands.*

"For Caesar." A legionnaire passed the *medicus* to Antinous.

"Did you bring his medicine?"

"As commanded. May I enter the tent?"

Antinous' brow furled at the wild look of the physician. His skin tone had a bluish tinge, and his robe was wet and hung off him. "Why are you wet?" He could not look away from the quite out-of-character man before him. The *medicus* had fire in his eyes. And it was not a passion to serve Caesar. Literal flames. Orbs ablaze.

"I rose from the Nile, Antinous."

"*Medicus?*"

"Let me attend Hadrian, and thereafter, we shall break words."

"You're not the physician."

"You can't call upon a god and expect not to be heard. We listen. Now, watch the sun rise and I'll return shortly."

Osiris.

The *medicus* chuckled. And within the guttural intonation, Antinous heard, "Yes."

Antinous burst forward, toppling his stool and barely missed the flames. *The gods heard me. My beloved shall live.*

A legionnaire approached. "Are you well, Antinous?"

"I am so very well. Thank you." He slipped inside Hadrian's tent.

Caesar reclined against his pillows; medicine vial raised. He tipped it to the physician. "To you, good sir, who brings me this pain-relieving draught."

"Of course, Caesar."

*

"I shall sleep." Hadrian shook off the dizziness blanketing him.

"I will see the good physician out," Antinous said softly. The *medicus* passed by him. The odor of the man's clothing had gone from horrendous to fresh like a breeze off the Nile. He whispered, "I know who you are."

The *medicus* turned to face Antinous once they were clear of the tent. The sun had just barely risen, and the heat of the day threatened the horizon. "I heard your prayer."

"Osiris."

"I can take the form of a mortal to communicate from time to time, but never before a *posca*-saturated physician."

"And my prayer?"

"He shall live until natural causes take him from this life."

Antinous took a deep breath. "What offering shall I make in gratitude?"

"I only accept one offering for answering a prayer such as this. I exact a heavy toll."

"Name it," Antinous replied.

"I want you."

"I am *his*."

"I will specify the time you shall ascend, Antinous. You shall become one with me and together we shall be remembered for a thousand years. Five thousand years."

"Am I to die?"

"You are to be resurrected as a god."

"I would stay with Hadrian."

"I have answered your prayer. Your offering has been accepted. And that offering is you."

"How long do I have?"

"Don't look at it as an end. Only your body shall cease. Your soul has an eternity ahead of it."

"I mean no disrespect, but please leave me to my thoughts. I will honor this sacrifice for I love Hadrian more than my own life. I shall not beg or bargain. I simply…need to think."

Osiris chuckled. "The *medicus* is about to lose his mind over my borrowing of his body, so I will depart. See you soon, Antinous, but not too soon."

Antinous startled as a bloodcurdling scream and the ring of hammers against metal sent waves of anguish and fear throughout. He knew what it was. The sounds of crucifixion were unmistakable. He wished inwardly that the practice would fall into disfavor. It was cruel. It was meant to be cruel. Then, an eerie hush fell over the entire encampment. An eerie silence as a great wooden X erected along the Nile to end the life of the traitor descended like a shroud. Crucifixion. Each arm and leg were spread and tied off, leaving the neck unable to support the weight of the head. Sometimes the convicted was nude. Sometimes bound tightly with reeds in delicate and sensitive places to prolong the agony of the torture. The spikes were heavy and made of highly polished copper. It was said the shine and glint of the sun off the alloy was to remind spectators as to whose light shone the brightest. Caesar's. All things returned to him. Hadrian preferred the X to the T-shaped structure. No need for a footrest to support the body and the X presented so much more frighteningly in his opinion. His predecessor, Trajan, had used the T.

Antinous set aside the bellyache and numbness permeating him as he contemplated the words of Osiris. *I am to die. So be it, but for now...I need to be at the execution. To prove I am a man in the eyes of Roman law. I should go. I must go.* He turned and vomited. He wiped his mouth and set out for the river's edge where a crowd had gathered. He strode large and furiously. With a purpose he'd rarely felt before. This was the advent of his citizenship and spectacular act to show his love. "Hold," he called.

The centurion ceased his hammer's blows. Antinous said nothing but took the small sledge from the soldier and without hesitation struck a blow to the copper spike protruding from the woman's wrist. An excited utterance washed through the crowd. The woman had long since passed out. He rose his arm to make a second blow and struck her in the head, opening her skull. He prayed she had died instantly.

He threw the hammer down. "Carry on." He spoke distinctly as he walked through the stunned audience to the execution. "I stand with Hadrian." The sound of the remaining three spikes being struck churned his stomach. *I stand with Hadrian.*

CHAPTER EIGHT

A ntinous' death blow ran through the camp like wildfire. Never had he been looked upon with fear and admiration. Violence was a way of life in the empire. He'd managed to stay off that path. Until now. He quickly entered Hadrian's tent to avoid the stares and wagging tongues. The news would travel faster than his legs could carry him. Violence and gossip were the vehicles upon which the empire thrived.

He took a long. "How do you fare, beloved?" He poured Hadrian a *posca* and then kneeled at his feet, offering the cup as a common slave might.

"You killed for me. Such news travels upon the breeze. I had not yet fallen asleep fully…and I heard your strike. And then the gossip."

"I did what I had to do to stay any further attempts on your life—or on mine. Ours is a deep and abiding love, but since I am not born of Rome, only its province, I am the shame of Caesar. I know this is not how you feel, nor truly I, but it is a true statement."

"When I adopt you, you will have the senate at your feet."

"Should we ever return to Italy, perhaps. I would rather stay here—in Egypt. I have seen the known world with you, Hadrian—but it is here—along the Nile, that I am most at home."

"I, too, love Egypt. Here we shall stay, Antinous. Though I am Caesar, I serve you."

"Don't tell the citizens that. They will revolt."

"I'm not afraid of the opinions of sheep. I am the wolf, after all."

Antinous had words at the tip of his tongue that he feared might disrupt Hadrian's mood, but they needed to be said. "I think, should you adopt me, I would further become a target. Perhaps make me your ward, not your son. I do not wish the power associated with your name. I want only your love."

Hadrian paused, appearing crestfallen. "As my heir, you will be protected more so than you are now. I could order an entire phalanx of the Pretorian guard to keep you safe."

"Yes, Caesar." *His mind is made up. I shall not survive to see his plans come to fruition. Should I tell him I bargained with Osiris—and was heard? Of all the times for a god to listen!* He pursed his lips in consideration. *No. I shall say nothing. His life is spared, and I am grateful my prayer has been answered. Though it means my death.* "Are you in pain, Hadrian?"

"Will you minister to me as a good physician, Antinous?"

"I will do what I must to keep you alive."

Hadrian pulled him up for a kiss. "I love you so, but I must sleep now. The draught has left me heady and tired. Will you hold me as I sleep?"

Antinous helped Hadrian to bed and then climbed in next to him. He wrapped his arms around Caesar, careful not to disturb the bandages. Then slept.

CHAPTER NINE

Hadrian had no issue fetching or pouring his own *posca*. It was tradition that bade him have a cupbearer. Moreover, this person had to be of strong character and one whose loyalty went unquestioned. It was a higher-status position than that of body servant. Since trust could be found nowhere in the empire, Hadrian was hesitant to accept the request that he follow prior emperors and travel with a cupbearer.

He had no problem bathing or dressing himself or even polishing his armor. The council claimed that as Caesar, others should do his bidding. Trajan had been even more independent than he and apparently that had set Rome's teeth on edge. And when Rome was not happy, people died. Senators. Divine emperors. Even the poorest of the citizenry suffered.

So, he dressed in his robes of state—a very odd

thing to do while moving with his army across Greece—and met with local governors to choose a new cupbearer. His former had been dismissed to attend to family business in Italy. This new bearer would undoubtedly be his constant companion, for moving an army across the globe was thirsty business.

"Your attendant must have grace and be fully vetted. He or she—"

Hadrian cut off the councilman. "He. I don't want a woman attending me."

"He must be articulate and educated and have a working knowledge of all areas of running a camp. He may act on your behalf from time to time with the daily duties of minding the troops and the camp followers."

Hadrian nodded. "A large task."

"And one that can only be appointed to the most loyal."

"Very well, how many await me?"

"I believe four, Caesar. Four Greek youths. More are there, but the females will be sent home upon our arrival."

"Ages?"

"The youngest is twelve or thirteen. The oldest is eighteen."

"Send anyone under eighteen away. Even if they've been educated in Italy at the teat of the senate, I have no interest. They are too young to be my companion, confidant, and bearer."

"Yes, Caesar. That will leave one. He is a wild young man who would rather hunt and fish than be groomed for the senate floor."

"I like him already."

As Caesar entered the pavilion where the potential cupbearers waited. He caught the tail end of all but one of them being scurried away. *Oh, dear gods…those children. I can't take a cup from a child's hands. I need a man. One with intellect and…* His train of thoughts paused as his gaze met that of the solitary applicant. *Beauty. Great beauty.* His focus turned entirely to the young man.

"I am Hadrian," he said softly.

"I am Antinous."

"Who is your father?"

"Sire, he is Claudios of Bythinia. A well-respected merchant."

"Are you his only son?"

"I have younger, Caesar."

"You have uncommon beauty for a youth. I find your look pleasant. You will suffice. Have you been educated, Antinous?"

"Yes. I spent time in Italy and Athens."

"Do you sing?"

"I do, Caesar, but…"

"Yes?" Hadrian's voice grew stern.

"I prefer the bow and hook to the niceties of court."

"As do I. Yes, you will do. Walk with me."

"Yes, Caesar."

Hadrian led Antinous from the pavilion and motioned for the guards and council to stay far behind them as he and his new cupbearer wandered the Bithynia shore. It was a solid port loaded with vessels sailing to and from Greece. A market had grown up by the docks and hawkers called their wares for all to hear.

"Are you hungry?" Hadrian asked.

"I am not, Caesar, but I am always willing to eat. My mother claims it to be a great foible of mine."

"I like a healthy appetite. What do you recommend? This is not my city."

Antinous motioned at a baker's stall. "He creates layer after layer of thin dough and mixes it with honey and nuts. That and a *posca* — most excellent."

Hadrian turned to his council. "Get us two of the baker's goods — the ones with thin layers, honey, and nuts and two *posca*. We shall sit by the dock and drink."

*

"Of course, Caesar." Antinous chose his words and actions carefully. This was a golden opportunity and a potential entrance to torments beyond compare. *This is the emperor! I am not a civilized youth with the etiquette and manners of a senator's son. I must be on my guard. I must make a good impression.*

They sat in the heat of the day, drinking the watered-down vinegar wine and eating the pastry. Though Hadrian was a very large, hairy man, his voice was soft and his demeanor far from frightening. Antinous listened to Caesar speak of adventures all around the empire. "Caesar, you seem to prefer the provinces to Rome."

"This is so, Antinous. I would rule from Egypt if the senators allowed it."

"You are the divine emperor of the Roman Empire. Can you not do as you wish?"

"Alas, I rule at the will of the senate. They

would have me conquering new lands, whilst I wish to secure the boundaries we have, thus keeping them strong and safe for my people. I have been a soldier. I have marched with legions. I have seen our borders grow and shrink like the turning of the moon. Today, Rome is as strong as ever she has been. I wish to preserve what we have."

"A solid plan, Caesar."

"As my companion, you need not agree with everything I say. I want opinions."

Antinous pulled his curls back and secured his hair with a leather strap from his wrist. "I do speak my mind, sir. That is why I am unmarried."

Hadrian laughed. "Oh, Antinous, you are amusing."

"It is true. My mother brought worthy women before me and I spurned them all, for I prefer running barefoot in the hills with my bow to the yoke of marriage."

"It is a yoke, indeed."

"Is that why your wife is not with you?"

"I married at the insistence of the senate. It is in name only. Vibia Sabina and I are second cousins and that is about as far as our relationship goes. I do not love her, nor she, me."

"Should you speak to me of such things, Caesar?"

"I will, Antinous. Your position is one of great importance. I may say things that need never be repeated and other things that I hope spread like wildfire around the camp. You will make certain I am not poisoned. You will be my most loyal companion. At night if I have needs, you will be there. If we are away from the camp, you will be my hearthstone."

"I am honored."

"You are of an age where I need not worry over you. The younger prospects—not a good fit. I have never enjoyed the company of very young boys or girls. Children are too precious to subject to the whims of wrinkled old bastards like me."

"I assure you, Caesar, you are quite fit and not at all wrinkled."

"Do you understand my meaning, Antinous?"

"It is commonplace for noblemen to take much younger boys than myself under their wing in education, and oft times, to bed. I believe you are saying you have never engaged in the act of love with someone younger than myself. Not of age."

"That is correct. Although I cannot abolish the practice, for it is deeply entrenched in our society, I am not one to groom a child."

"Do you have a lover, Caesar?" Antinous tingled as Hadrian's brown eyes gazed into his and penetrated his soul. He barely heard the reply for the beating of his heart.

"Not yet."

"When you take a woman to your bed, I shall make myself scarce, unless it is your desire I watch."

"I do not take women. I have, on occasion, taken a beautiful young man." Hadrian paused. "But none were as beautiful as you...Antinous."

Antinous again trembled as Hadrian touched his arm. *Our divine emperor will take me to his bed. I know it. Thank all the gods, for I would spend every moment alone with my hand on my cock and thoughts of him filling my head.* "Thank you, Caesar."

"Please, call me Hadrian. It is your right as my companion."

"Hadrian." Antinous gingerly reached up an placed his fingertips over the emperor's, whose hand still rested on his arm. "Hadrian."

"You must understand that whether or not you come to me in the night, your job as cupbearer is secure. I have never taken a servant by force, nor abused the slave of another. I do not keep slaves. All under my tent are paid for their time. I do not whore, either. Many a young man has approached me with offers of love for pay, but I refuse them all. Prostitution is a noble profession, but I do not partake."

Antinous could barely speak. The words caught in his throat. "Yes, Caesar."

"Have you made love?"

Antinous nodded. "With males and females and once with a person who was both."

"And?"

Antinous cast his gaze down and looked up through his lashes. "I prefer the touch of males, Hadrian."

"As our relationship continues and we become accustomed to each other, will you have me?"

"Yes, Caesar. Hadrian. When that time arrives, I will come to you in the night."

Hadrian chuckled and squeezed Antinous' hand. "Bring *posca* with you. At that time."

* * * *

Adrian awakened in a cold sweat, buckled over

in pain. He immediately looked at his phone. Only an hour had passed. "What the hell was that?" He stood and stretched. "How did I end up prone against an overturned chair?" He touched his ribcage. Pain shot through his solar plexus. He pulled back his T-shirt to find a horribly bruised torso. A great healed gash ran from side to belly. "Well, that's new." He traced his fingertips along the scar. It had not healed cleanly. The stitches used to close it had been large. Too large. *I do not recall such a wound being struck.* He stood and walked around his apartment. He flipped on the light and noticed another oddity. He wore a ring on his right index finger. An old ring. Brass. No. "This is gold." He pulled it off to examine it more thoroughly. "This is a Hadrianic coin fashioned into a ring. This is the great seal of Caesar. I do not own such a treasure. I could never afford it. It is perfect. Mint. And it must be nineteen hundred years old."

Adrian swooned and sunk into an overstuffed chair. He spoke into the empty room. "What just happened to me?" He took a deep breath and thought back on the vision imparted to him after melding with the spirit. The bruise. The scar. The ring. He glanced at his shorts. A semen stain and the overwhelming presence that he'd just had sex. "Well...that was certainly realistic. I dreamed of Hadrian and Antinous in situations not recorded in history, but easily presumed, and now have the marks and leavings of those events on my body." He leaned forward to allow blood flow to his head. Something his mother had taught him. "This can't be real. Did I hit my head? Am I still asleep?"

He pushed himself to his feet and then

stretched. It was almost eight in the morning. *Time to get up, anyway. All right, Antinous…today is your day. October* 30th. He wanted to dress professionally because of the tours to the church. It was little more than a hole-in-the-wall shop—but its significance was very important to his tour. Especially today. *This is the day you became a god.*

Adrian donned white linen walking shorts, a blue shirt, and hat. He wore sneakers. He put a small vial of water and another of salt into his pocket. He reached for the handful of coins on his nightstand. Traditional offerings to the god when visiting the temple. He had included the information on offerings in the brochure. However, most of the souls visiting on October 30th were already adherents and knew the drill, though his morning tour had some bona fide tourists from the Midwest. His profit margin tripled this time of year. Today he would make two trips to the site of the drowning and ruins of Antinoöpolis. The first tour began at the church, then a stop at El-Minya, where the ruins of Antinoöpolis were located, then the pyramids. The second would begin at Giza near the pyramids and end at the church. He had an employee who would return the first tour group to Cairo while he escorted the second. "Hail Antinous."

I don't worship. I am not spiritual. I am not sexual. I am…not worthy of ghostly visits or spirit encounters.

You are more worthy now than ever you were. My divinity sees through your humanity, and I would embrace you.

Adrian didn't see the spirit speaking to him, but certainly felt its presence. *I can't do this! Please stop!*

Is that truly your desire, or would you rather explore the pleasure of submitting to my spiritous actions?

"I'm afraid." It was the truth. "And we need to have a conversation about consent. It's important."

I am with you, and I am a god. You have nothing to fear. Nothing to lose, but everything to explore. Please…tell me about consent.

"To share such an intimate experience with me requires that I agree to it first. That's consent. In a nutshell."

Are you injured? Frightened terribly?

Adrian shook his head. "I don't understand what has transpired. To what was I witness?"

Antinous' spiritous voice grew calm and the very air around Adrian seemed to warm and fragrant. "Us."

Adrian startled, for this time the reply was audible—not only in his mind. *Us?* "I have to work."

"Trust me, Adrian. Once reunited with your past, you will have no regrets."

"Antinous."

"It is I."

Adrian swallowed hard. "Antinous. On this auspicious day I am being blessed by a god. I want to believe it."

"Then do."

"When you say the very real vision I experienced…was us…what do you mean, exactly?"

"Do I have your consent to continue? To make things known to you that are already a part of your hidden world. I can draw things from your past to the present and then…everything will be clear."

Adrian was a man who trusted his gut. He trusted his abilities and experiences. *This feels right.* "Yes." A moment of panic rushed in—soon calmed by a reassuring presence that he was all right. That it would be all right. That warmth grew hot until every part of his body seemed to stand under the Egyptian noonday sun. Perspiration trickled from his brow. "What is it you need from me?" The words stuck in his throat. He glanced at the ring and felt the pain of the wounds on his ribs. Warm arms encircled him. "I am not Hadrian."

Soft lips pressed against the back of his neck. "You are he."

Adrian didn't turn. "And if I am, then what? It's not as if we live on the same plain of existence. From what I understand a ghost and mortal..."

"I am returned."

"What?"

"I have returned to you that we may live together once more along the Nile, making love and hunting and fishing and commanding all we see."

"This is the twenty-first century. There is no game and the Nile is polluted. There is so much plastic filling it that it will take decades for it to recover."

"Then we shall make love."

Adrian turned. Strong arms encircled him, and he instinctively wrapped his around the shoulders of the beautiful being before him. "If you are reborn, how can you come to me in this form?"

"I am a god."

"And I am not."

"I would forgo divinity to be with Hadrian

again. His soul rests within you, and on this momentous day, I implore you to allow our journey to continue that you may come to know our shared past."

"I have two tours today. Important ones."

"You never need toil in the marketplace again. I am with you."

"Let's discuss this after the tours." *I'll think about this later.*

"I shall be with you."

"I need everything I have—everything I am...intact today, Antinous." Saying the name aloud tasted like honey upon his lips. "No ethereal visions, all right?"

Antinous nodded. "Of course, but I will join your tour."

"You are not dressed for the part."

"My reincarnation agent has educated me on modern attire so I can walk amongst the peoples of this place without drawing too much attention."

"A reincarnation agent?" Adrian pocketed his keys.

"Yes. She's watching. In truth, as I made the journey between lives I was inundated with great quantities of information, and as a god, I absorbed it all. Languages. Electricity. The utter insanity of religion and politics this modern era brings. My agent is monitoring the timeline to see if it explodes since I chose to return in a way most untoward. I never was one to follow convention. I waited a very long time to reincarnate because I refused to be reborn from the body of a woman and then wait decades to be with you. I am divine. I have reincarnated thusly. I swore that I would only return to your arms in a form we would both find agreeable. I've waited quite some time."

"Isn't that confusing?"

"Yes. It is a bit."

"This is nuts, Antinous. You're rewriting time and space."

"I assure you I have not lost my mind. You are my beloved reincarnated and we shall explore our past together while we create our future."

"I'm asexual. I don't have relations. Forgoing such things has simplified my life."

"I shall convince you otherwise—with your consent. I know in your heart that I appeal to you, just as you do me. We will be happy together. The twenty-first century shall embrace us."

Adrian bristled at the thought of developing a relationship. Any relationship. He kept his cool. "What shall I call you? Do you wish to continue using Antinous as your name?"

"I think I shall be known as Alexander. Will that suffice?"

"Do you have money? Where will you live? I'm not ready to share my apartment much less my bed."

"From what I gather, I have everything—even a luxury hotel room overlooking the pyramids of Giza. And what a nasty bit of work has been done to them! Why there are houses and dining establishments nearly to their bases and the pollution here is awful. There is a flatbread restaurant overlooking them. It says pizza is Italian, but I know Italian food and Pizza Hut is not a proper Roman food."

"Welcome to Cairo."

CHAPTER TEN

Adrian finished getting ready for work after the semi-corporeal specter of Antinous departed. Two tours on the busiest tourist day of the year for him atop a randy romp in another realm with Antinous, himself, that had left him bruised and bejeweled. *Thank all the gods I can compartmentalize. I don't think I could be the cheery tour guide today without putting all that a literal ghost has said to me in the background for a bit. I've never considered reincarnation before. I've never considered having such profound actions take place in the spirit realm that I awaken marked. And sated. I came. A wet dream, perhaps. Or I really did fuck the shit out of Antinous along the Nile, in another time, in another space.*

As always, the narrow streets of Old Cairo were loud and busy. A large souk was near his apartment complex, and if the wind blew just right, the fragrant scents of exotic herbs and spices filled the air. Today was such a day. His senses were kissed by cumin, coriander, cardamom, chili, aniseed, bay leaves, ginger, cinnamon, and cloves. Dates, figs, fine cheeses, and coffee perfumed the breeze. He didn't take tourists to the vast marketplace of stalls and kiosks. Pickpockets were rampant. However, today would be the best day to show them—no—surround them, by the best of Cairo. *I'll suggest they visit – with a caveat against the rolling teams of thieves.*

He drove his minibus to the pick-up location at a hotel. He had six a.m. attendees. He owned a twelve-person van that had once been his home but was now converted to a slick tour bus with air conditioning, a cooler, and even a camp shower if someone got heat stroke. Each tourist paid over three hundred US dollars for the excursion to the church, the site of Antinoöpolis, and the pyramids. He counted seven in attendance—the seventh being a fair-haired young man with piercing blue eyes and a regal bearing.

"Hello."

Antinous. In fully mortal form. Dear gods, he's lovely. No wonder Hadrian proclaimed him divine. I would have done the same should he have died in my arms. His beauty rivals the lotus and the constellation named for him. "Hello."

Graceful and soft-spoken, Antinous leaned forward and whispered to Adrian, "I look much like I did in life. Does this form appeal to you?"

Adrian nodded. "You are very handsome." He turned his attention to the others. "We begin at the temple and end at the pyramids, where another transport will return you to Cairo while I conduct the evening tour. I'd like to thank you all for coming—especially today." He glanced at Antinous. "It should be a special day along the Nile. One to remember."

"Thank goodness for air conditioning," one of the tourists remarked.

"We have plenty of water. Help yourself. It is a hot autumn day in Egypt," Adrian replied. "I lived in this van for a while when I first moved to Cairo. It has a shower too. Just in case. And I've a handful of new kaftans if you all fall in the mud." Adrian chuckled.

Antinous laughed. "I love Egypt. It is the time of inundation, and the weather can be unpredictable, but always hot. Why, I recall a time when rain fell from the sky and rose up as steam from the white blocks of the sphinx."

The same tourist spoke out. "How many times have you visited, son?"

"I lived here for quite some time. Years ago."

"You don't look older than twenty. Your parents live here?"

"No. My parents are Greek. I…came here for a job. Then fell in love and stayed."

"Where's your lady friend now?"

Antinous looked at the tourist and without hesitation replied, "I am gay." He motioned toward Adrian. "That is the correct word, is it not?"

Adrian nodded.

The red-faced tourist settled back into his seat. "Well, good for you."

Antinous frowned. "Is this how things are accepted now? With indifference?"

"If you're lucky, sure. Sometimes non-traditional lifestyles are an uphill battle."

"The gods of Egypt and Rome are no longer worshipped here, are they? I recall that Abrahamic faiths have taken precedence. Is it within those faiths that being gay is taboo?"

Adrian nodded. "Often, but love is love. And that is a plain and simple truth."

"I loved Hadrian."

"I know."

Antinous continued. "This is the anniversary of my death. I feel the pull of the Nile, my lungs burning as they filled, and the blackness of death overtake me. He was my last thought before I passed into the arms of the underworld."

"He held you in his arms along the bank of the Nile and wept. Caesar wept. His overt display of mourning was not well accepted by Rome. Many who wished him to be a more active husband to Vibia Sabina ridiculed him harshly, but in that grief, you became legend."

"I became a god."

"Your influence still holds after nearly two thousand years. Statues, poems, admirers—even a constellation and a flower."

"The statues make me too young in appearance. I assure you I had pubic hair when Hadrian and I began our life together. I think, perhaps, that the sculpturers of the day merely worked with tradition and not reality. It was the Greek style for art. Hadrian did not have boy lovers."

"I saw that—in the dream."

"It wasn't a dream, Adrian. It was a real. I took you *there*."

"You are called *beautiful boy* by many. And right now, it's better I do not dwell on this time travel romance you've set in motion."

"I was a man. I am a man."

"But you are beautiful."

"I believe that we can choose to live here—or then. I'm not quite certain of all the parameters yet."

"My life is here," Adrian replied.

"Then, if you will have me—after whatever courtship is necessary in this era—my life shall be here too."

CHAPTER ELEVEN

Adrian tuned out the chatter of his guests as his driver sped through the streets to the Cairo Church of Antinous. The lifeforce radiating from Antinous nearly had him gobsmacked. He tried to listen to the tonal inflections of a question from the others in order to be an accommodating guide, but truly, was lost in the aura of a god. He pulled his thoughts away from those self-depreciating ones of self-loathing and lack of self-worth. *If I am Hadrian reincarnated, then within me is all he was. The strength of Rome and love beyond measure. I am being given a gift. The gift of a lifetime. Of a dozen lifetimes. Please don't be a trickster god. Please.*

The temple of Antinous was small and built into the side of an alley in Old Cairo. It had a nondescript sign in three languages — Egyptian Arabic, English, and Greek. "Church of Antinous." The chief priest lived in a tidy apartment above the sanctuary and kept a low profile. A homosexual in Egypt...there was need to be secretive. Though not expressly unlawful under Egyptian law, certain groups did not express acceptance. The priest ran a performing arts troupe, which reenacted the events of Antinous' death along the Nile—very close to where Hadrian was said to have pulled the body of his lover ashore. It was quite a passion play.

Adrian put on his game face and led the tourists into the building. "And this is the Cairo Antinous temple. Songs are sung and his story retold in this place. A candle is lit 24/7 and the priest and a few others make their way to the shrine at *El-Shaikh Ebada* to make offerings." Adrian reverently left the small vials of salt and water at the offering table by the door. "Because of the significance of today's date, they will perform a passion play—a reenactment of Antinous' death and subsequent deification. There's really nothing left of the original city. Everything was torn down to create other structures. Napoleon did a number on it. We can see the shrine and the outline of what the great circus of Antinoöpolis was once. Long ago. There are, naturally, beautiful mosques and some interesting apartments overlooking the Nile. Not a huge population. Street vendors. It's a mud city—but the ruins of Antinoöpolis do exist. Oh, and should you come here at night. A telescope has been set up on the roof that one may catch sight of the constellation Aquila, which is the modern-day constellation of Antinous."

"Welcome! We offer water and prayers to Antinous, and he is remembered." It was the priest.

He wore a simple white kaftan without adornment. "I am Nasser, priest of Antinous. Would you like to hear a prayer?"

The tour group murmured positively. Adrian moved next to Antinous, who whispered, "Well, I do hope the prayer is succinct. I've never been a god to demand elaborate ceremonies." Adrian hushed him.

Nasser raised his arms and said softly, melodically, "To our divine Antinous, we give our prayers and thanks. May all be blessed by him, the beautiful, just, and benevolent. May he forever dwell in our hearts and minds." He paused. "Yes, it is simple, but Antinous doesn't need too much pomp. We remember him by our actions. By whom we honor and who we love. He was the most important person in Hadrian's life. He was lover and god."

Antinous whispered, "Hail Hadrian, divine emperor."

Adrian didn't look up but quickly squeezed Antinous/Alexander's hand.

Nasser continued, "I urge you to sit quietly in this place and consider the vast contributions of Antinous and Hadrian. Why, the two were influential in ways that have continued for nearly two thousand years. Have you questions?"

A member of Adrian's group rose his hand and spoke, "Antinous is the gay god. The god of homosexual love. Of healing. Of those who put others' needs before their own. He gave his life for Hadrian—or at least that is one belief surrounding his death."

Antinous spoke up. "It is true. He gave his life to

ensure Hadrian would not feel the blade of assassination. He bargained with Osiris at the Nile's edge and the price was his life. As he died, he was lifted on high by the Nile god, and by Caesar's own words, proclaimed divine. There, in that state of non-substantiality between life and death, Antinous waited for Hadrian's return through reincarnation that they might once again live and love on this mortal plain. He waited nearly two thousand years."

Nasser laughed. "Indeed! Hail Osiris-Antinous! I believe as you, sir. So great was his love for Hadrian that he gave his own life. Though I do not know of Antinous' reincarnation—or Hadrian's— but wouldn't that be miraculous and the stuff of legends?"

Adrian chimed in. "Some believe Antinous was intoxicated and fell from the barge where he and Hadrian toured the Nile."

"That is an appalling scenario," Alexander replied. "And false. It is as completely ridiculous as to say he was eaten by Nile crocodiles."

Adrian sighed. "No one knows for certain."

"Then every historian and scribe shall, heretofore, be instructed to record the truth that future generations will know of Hadrian's love and Antinous' long wait in the shadow lands. He refused to reincarnate—though he was given several opportunities. If Hadrian was not already reborn and ready to accept the return of his lover, Antinous refused to return. He would not settle to be reborn as an infant and have Hadrian grow old without him."

"You have quite a mythos developed, friend."

Nasser laughed. "It is welcome, as are all stories and experiences with our Antinous. Those experiences are referred to as UPG or unverifiable personal gnosis. They are valid in our eyes."

Adrian spoke up, "We shall see Nasser at the Nile for the recreation of Antinous' ascension. We have a little more time here. I encourage you to enjoy the paintings adorning the walls and perhaps purchase a book compiled by Nasser and the temple. There's a coffee bar next door. Meet outside in thirty minutes." He turned to Antinous. "You, come with me."

Nasser held out his hand to Antinous. "Sir, you are known to me."

"How so?"

Adrian, nervous, sidled in close to Antinous.

"You look like my god. I see him in you."

"The depictions of Antinous are familiar to me, and it has been remarked before the strong resemblance I bear the god. Good genes."

"Remarkable. Will I see you at the Nile's edge?"

"He'll be there," Adrian said, pulling Antinous outside. He sequestered Antinous in the vestibule of a closed shop. "I have always believed myself to be an open-minded guy, but you here—like this— and having memories that are not mine—and the sex and the wound…I'm about to have a meltdown. I worked as a trauma nurse for ten years and I know how to compartmentalize shit. This, however, is blowing my mind."

"Ah, you were a healer. Far more spectacular occupation than when you were a laundress. Adrian, I have little experience in the shapeshifting abilities of godhood, but I can adapt. Whatever is easier for you to accept. Would you prefer a woman? If Hadrian and I are together, gender doesn't really matter. Everything will make sense. I assure you."

"I am not Hadrian."

"You were. If you wish, I can give you the identities of everyone into whom you've reincarnated over the last two thousand years. You were a laundress in 14th century France. Died of the plague. They didn't find your body for over a week. Let's see...you died in 1820 in the very early years of the American Civil War too. That was again by disease. Dysentery. Hadrian has reincarnated with some avoidance of politics or power. Perhaps his reign as Caesar soured him on being in charge."

"I am not Hadrian. If I was, then so be it."

"How can I convince you?"

Adrian took a deep breath. "After the tours...take me on another journey. To Libya. To when you and Hadrian killed the lion. To Hadrian's wall, perhaps."

"I was at the wall briefly with my beloved in AD 122. Then we set out for other realms. Britannia is a cold, damp, and dark place. The wall promised to bring security and trade in that wild place."

"To the lion then."

"He was a bristling thing. Angry. I think rabid with rage. Hadrian struck him, and though we were on horseback, that lion attacked. That lion was so aroused with life and death that when I struck him down, he tore Hadrian's horse and the emperor's thigh."

"I will see that battle."

"You may come away with further scars."

"If I do, then I accept that I am the reincarnation of Hadrian and that you…you waited for me for two thousand years."

"I could have returned at any time, but circumstances were poor. I was not interested in being a homesteader or washwoman. I love the Nile. I had to wait until you, Adrian Alcaraz, a kind man of Spanish descent, born in a place called New Hampshire and now living and working in Cairo, made your appearance."

"I never knew my father. I got his name and that's about it. He died shortly after my birth. My mother never remarried."

"I'm sure you come from good stock."

Adrian laughed. "That's what my mother always said."

Antinous leaned in for a kiss. "I want you, my love."

Adrian hesitated. *I do not seek physical relationships.* He pressed his lips against Antinous'—for a moment. "This is new to me."

"Have you laid with a man?"

Adrian nodded. "And women. I used to be omnisexual. I loved who I was with. I've been with lots of people—sometimes it seems all of them at the same time. It eventually wore me out and I became who I am today—*uninvolved.* It wasn't healthy."

"My reincarnation agent said you were prone to a solitary life. That you did not find attraction in others."

"My past behaviors were not conducive to lasting relationships and brought only suffering. I needed to make changes from my attitude on down. I did. I'm happier now."

"Do you never want to fall in love?"

"Being in love for more than three weeks at a time would be exceptional. I've never experienced it."

"Perhaps when you embrace the part of you that is Hadrian you will also grasp the deepest nature of true love."

"We can speak of this later. I need to keep frosty for the tour." Adrian paused. "I believe you are who you say you are. You are a spiritous being returned to Earth in some alternative form of reincarnation. You look like Antinous. I have parasomnia injuries, and this ring."

"It is good to assess all that has transpired and that which is yet to come."

"Antinous, I think this will take some time."

"I am a god. Time is my ally."

Adrian didn't reply. He refocused his attention to the tour and loaded the van.

CHAPTER TWELVE

e depressed the PA system call button. "When we reach *Sheik Abada*, the ruins of Antinoöpolis are very close by and you are welcome to walk the ruins at your leisure. Although I am leery of street vendors, they will be out *en force*—especially today—with Antinous-related trinkets. Some may sell olive leaves and fruit that can be left as offerings. Others may have delightful little plastic statues of Antinous that are made in China for the Egyptian tourist trade. We'll have about an hour at the site before the ceremony and then a three-hour drive to the pyramids."

"Antinous is not fond of plastic. Any other offering would be well-received."

"Thank you, sir—for your continued UPG of the gay god."

"You're welcome."

"Will there be lunch?" another tourist asked. A

large man with a red face, fishing cap, and Bermuda shorts. "I'm diabetic."

Antinous replied, "There is a Pizza Hut quite near Giza."

"As stated on the itinerary, Mr. Raymond, a light lunch will be provided during our visit to the ruins. When we reach the pyramids, we'll have a box-lunch style dinner, and you will meet the bus taking you back to the city while I do the evening tour. And on that bus, adult beverages are allowed."

"Hallelujah," Mr. Raymond said. The others laughed.

Antinous turned in his seat to face Mr. Raymond. "What means hallelujah? I do not know this word."

"Well, son...it's a praise word. It's a way to thank God for little things. In this case, beer on the bus."

"Which god?"

"The only God."

"There are many gods. Why, I—"

Adrian cut Antinous off. "If you look closely, just off in the distance facing east, is the ruins of an obelisk. Some scholars believe it may have originally been erected as a marker at the entrance to Antinoöpolis."

The driver slowed the van, then stopped at a pre-planned vantage point suitable for photos.

"At one time, this obelisk stood at the center of a racetrack. Chariot races. Can you imagine the spectacle? Devotees of Antinous flocked to the races. Though Hadrian's health declined after Antinous' death, I'm sure he was here from time to time. He returned to Tivoli—and constructed another obelisk and surrounded himself with images of his lost love. At one time, it is estimated that in this area alone, there were over a hundred statues of his lover and god."

Antinous agreed. "Theirs was a love to last the ages. So deeply in love were they the world vanished when they were in each other's arms. Nothing mattered to Antinous, except Hadrian's embrace. And to Hadrian, Antinous was the air he breathed."

"And stars," Adrian added. "The constellation, now called Aquilla. And if you look along the east bank of the Nile, you may see a blush-colored lotus that is named for Antinous. It sprang from the spot where Hadrian held his lover's corpse and blooms in honor of Osiris-Antinous."

"You are waxing poetic, sir."

"Yes, Ms. Blakely. I do that from time to time. Antinous had a huge impact on history. Stars, flowers, an asteroid, a crater on one of Jupiter's moons, even a blue spider. He was a young man from modern-day Turkey, a Greek citizen, but not yet formalized as a Roman citizen, potentially the heir of Hadrian and half of one of the world's greatest love stories. Oh, and there is poetry—notably by Fernando Pessoa."

"Can we get closer to the ruins?"

"Of course. Driver?"

Across the desert and nearer the Nile stood the ruins. Dusty, dry, impressive in their once vast magnificence. "His name is inscribed in hieroglyphics here. And there was hope that a dig would reveal a lost temple."

"That spot is farther ahead." Antinous pointed north of their location. "Not too far. The city was built where it was because the ground was better suited for it. The flood waters don't come this high."

Reynolds chimed in. "How do you know that lad?"

Antinous smiled politely at the tourist. "Research."

Adrian continued, "There is a cistern, columns, remains of roadways. And the spirit of Antinous resides in this place. At Abada—I feel him far less for the hustle and bustle and plastic trinkets. I'd like to add that the cult of Coptic Mary also has claim to this area. At some point, ruins of Antinous' city were deliberately buried. Either by that cult or perhaps as crops were planted. We have about an hour here, so please explore. Points of interest are listed in the guidebook I provided."

"Getting mystical on us there, bud?"

"Yes, Mr. Reynolds. My love of Roman history took me to understand a deep connection to the story of Hadrian and Antinous. Sometimes the way I feel in this place is…mystical."

"Can't fault you for that. I'm more of a battlefields tour kind of guy, but the Mrs. here likes romance novels and she's the one who wanted to do this tour. It has been inspiring for us both." He playfully elbowed his wife in the ribs. "If you know what I mean."

She slapped his arm away. "Behave."

Adrian's cell chirped. He stepped away from the group. "You go on now. Explore!" He answered his phone. "Yes?"

"Adrian, it is I, Nasser. My vehicle is delayed in

a long line at a checkpoint. The actors and I...we cannot make the first reenactment. It is the oddest thing. It seems an item was stolen from the museum and all cars are being searched."

"What was stolen?"

"His name, Adrian. The name *Antinous*. The slab from Antinoöpolis bearing the hieroglyphs of his name. On this day, of all days—someone has chosen to steal his very essence and his connection to Osiris and the place where he was deified."

Because he's here in the flesh? Is this a timeline glitch? "Wow. All right. I can pitch hit. I have someone here who knows the story well and he and I can...act it out. I have a couple of robes in the van, and why I haven't taken it out I'll never know...a *subligaria*."

"To be honest to the scene, Adrian, you should be nude."

"No one wants to see that."

"You would be surprised what is considered beautiful."

Adrian glanced at Antinous. *Yes. Beautiful.* "I got this, my friend. Call me when you get out of the snarl. Maybe the evening tour will see your actors nude along the Nile." He ended the call and turned to Antinous, who had not moved too far away.

"Want to help me save this tour?"

Antinous laughed. "Of course."

"The reenactment players will be quite delayed. How would you feel about drowning again?"

"Ah. You and I shall be the actors of my demise. I can assure you, I know exactly what happened, but do you?"

Adrian nodded. "Historically speaking, yes."

"What of the events in your heart? Do you recall Hadrian sinking into the mud at the Nile's edge, holding my lifeless body? He wept bitterly. He wanted to die. It was then Osiris planted a seed of life in his mind. And I was proclaimed a god by the living deity of the Roman Empire. My body breathed no longer but my spirit was exalted, and I rose into the heavens."

"Coach me."

"I can do better than that." Antinous reached for Adrian's hand and guided him into the mists of the past again.

CHAPTER THIRTEEN

Sailing south on the Nile, going from the Upper to the Lower Kingdom was a welcome respite from the drudgery and dust of the encampment. It wasn't his barge—he'd borrowed one from an Egyptian nobleman and friend of the empire. It was an amazing vessel. Flat bottomed with a large center sail and a dozen oarsmen. It provided shade for guests as they lounged and had room for servants and even a cook.

"This is the life, eh, Antinous?"

"Wherever we have roamed, Caesar, I have considered that place heaven, but truly, the breeze I feel now has been sent by the gods. How smoothly we glide along the swollen Nile. Why even the crocodiles are docile in our wake."

"I'm glad you like it." Hadrian stretched out his arms. "Come here."

Antinous gladly fell against the emperor's chest and sought his eager mouth. They kissed passionately, without thought for whom might stand witness. The servants certainly didn't care. Only a senator might raise an eyebrow — and they were far away.

"I love you, Antinous. You are my air. My oasis. My first cup of *posca* after a long day with my troops. You are my staff along this most perilous journey as Caesar and divine Emperor of Rome. My borders begin and end with you. Outside those secure borders I shall not travel unless you are by my side."

Antinous pressed his lips against Hadrian's. "I love you. I always will."

Hadrian chuckled. "Perhaps I shall entreat the gods to fashion us into stars that we may shine forever."

"Yes. Wherever we are together, is home. Be it here — on this glorious barge along the Nile — or in the night sky."

"Fill our cups, Antinous."

Antinous rose and then poured two cups of *posca*. "To our love." He passed a cup to Caesar, and they drank the vinegared wine. "Hadrian, this wine is the most bitter thing in our lives. I am so very blessed by your love."

"Offer the oarsmen a cup, Antinous. Let us all celebrate this much needed respite from the day-to-day grind of soldiering. Five days have we to relax and revel in this sacred time of the Nile's flood. We can make offerings to Hapi and Osiris. Pour a *posca* over the side for the gods."

"Perhaps the gods will not enjoy the wine of

soldiers. We should offer something of a higher grade. Have we any *mulsum*? Let's give the gods something sweet and spicy."

"Clever lad. Currying favor with fine offerings." Hadrian laughed.

Antinous poured cups of *posca* and then handed them to the men on the oars. The barge floated a bit—though the lack of oars to water did not make a particular difference, for they were experienced Roman sailors who understood the phrase *smooth sailing*. They were at a narrow point in the great length of the river. During its inundation, it ballooned as if pregnant in some areas and closed in others as if it had delivered. The Nile's waters brought life to Egypt. Sacred river. Sacred flood.

Hadrian laid back on his settee and opened his arms to embrace Antinous. His wide reach and broad chest made for a potent hug—strong and arousing. Antinous kissed his throat. "Your touch awakens my body."

"Oh?" Hadrian slid his hand inside his lover's *subligaria*. "I see. Perhaps it is the breeze off the water and the wine that has made you so…hard."

"No, my love. It is being with you. Flesh to flesh. Your scent intoxicates."

"Would you like more *posca*?"

"I've already had three cups. This wine is stronger than usual."

"Nothing but the best for you." Hadrian encircled Antinous' penis with his thick fingers and pulled. "Come for me, my love."

Antinous tossed his head back and thrust his hips to meet Hadrian's grasp. He closed his eyes and reveled in the sensation. Until he opened them.

"Oh, Hadrian. Look!"

"Now?"

"Priests of Osiris in ritual."

"Forgive me, Antinous. I do wish to see that. We shall continue soon." Hadrian rose and went to the edge of the barge. "Ah…they perform an opening of the eyes on Osiris' statue. How rare a spectacle."

Antinous couldn't reply. His focus was directed solely on the eyes of the statue, which were newly painted white. He felt the effigy's gaze penetrate him. He shuddered. *I am violated by the will of Osiris. I am called to his service, though it means I must leave Hadrian. Do I regret my pact? No. I regret nothing. Hadrian will die an old man in his bed and not at the hands of an assassin or by some wasting disease.* Antinous called to the god. And found the god waiting. *Is it time, my lord?*

It is time, Antinous. Divinity flowed through Osiris' voice as it echoed in Antinous' mind and heart.

The voice reminded him of the wind whistling through the sands. *So soon?*

Yes.

How am I to die?

The Nile shall swallow you. Your lungs shall fill, and your life shall end. Within the moment between light and darkness, you shall be raised on high and given divinity.

By you.

It will be by Caesar's decree and by my hands you are made.

I fear he will never be the same…after my demise.

Drink your wine and make love to your mate. And when the Nile reaches for you, embrace her. Be one with the flood. In inundation comes renewal.

"I shall honor our agreement," Antinous whispered.

"Of course you shall," Hadrian replied. "Is this not marvelous? Painted priests in their linen robes, opening the eyes of their god and blessing his name and the lifegiving flood waters. I'm very glad to have witnessed this."

It is not to you, my love, that I replied but to Osiris at the hour of my death. And my rebirth. "Yes, as am I." Antinous took a few steps so he was under the canopy again and then poured *posca*. He drank it quickly. Then poured another. "Hail Osiris, god of agriculture who brings life to the desert." He raised the cup and emptied it with three large gulps.

"My love, the wine and the spectacle along with the gentle roll of this barge would see me sleep for a bit. Will you lay with me?"

"Of course." Antinous crawled in between Hadrian's arms, his back to Caesar's belly. It was warm and comforting. And he knew it was his last time. He snuggled in, desirous of capturing the moment. *Something I can take with me. Something to recall for all time. Hadrian's body against mine. Me, in his arms. There is no greater love than ours.* In the distance, the priests of Osiris called their prayers over the water. Lifegiving water soon to close around him and send him to his next great adventure. *If only I could take Hadrian with me…*

Antinous rose from the settee and stood at the prow of the ship. The oarsmen were asleep. Night had fallen. The anchor dropped. The sky was a million pinpoints of light and their reflection on the Nile made it appear as though two million stars stood witness to his actions. *What I do now, I do for Hadrian and to honor Osiris.* He turned to take one last look at his sleeping love.

He silently went over the edge. No struggle. No indecision. Without hesitation, he allowed the Nile to fill his lungs and take him. The burning desperation subsided quickly when he opened himself to the flood.

Everything went dark.

No stars.

No reflection.

No embrace.

No life.

CHAPTER FOURTEEN

Dawn did not break tranquil and calm. The energy on the barge grew chaotic as Hadrian realized Antinous was not in his arms, nor on the boat. He tore through the furnishings and awakened the servants to question them. "What did you see? Where is Antinous?" No one had seen anything. "He was drinking. Did he fall overboard? If he did, even after several cups of *posca*, I'm certain he could swim. Antinous is a strong swimmer."

The oarsmen and servants on the barge cowered in fear as the emperor raged. Hadrian was a large, loud, angry, panicked man. "I should kill you all for allowing this!" Caesar's wrath at his empty arms tore the barge apart. Exhausted, Hadrian did not punish them. He sank to his knees and covered his face with his hands as if praying.

By all the gods, where is he? He steeled his nerves

and pushed the dire emotional ache in the pit of his stomach down deep. *I am Caesar. I am the voice of the gods on Earth. They will not take my love from me. They cannot do this terrible thing.* Hadrian scanned the length and width of the barge, and then spotted the body of his lover tangled in reeds on the east bank. His throat grew dry, and he trembled as he commanded the rowers to pull the barge toward the reeds.

Though thirty seconds from command to stroke had passed, he could not wait. He would not wait. *Too slow!* Hadrian dove into the Nile and swam to Antinous. *He must live. He must live!* But he knew Antinous no longer drew breath. As he lifted his head between strokes, fighting tears and withholding insane panic, he saw the pallor of death on his beloved. And there was blood. Blood in the water from a gash across Antinous' forehead. *He fell in and hit his head. He drowned.* He reached the body and carefully pulled him ashore. *Antinous is dead.*

Hadrian waded through the thick mud, pushing aside the reeds and lotuses until solid ground was beneath his feet. He swaddled Antinous in his arms. He held him close and rocked. He kissed the cold lips and stroked the bloodied, muddied hair. "Live," he begged. "Live."

Antinous had no pulse. No breath. No warmth. Black hollows hid glassy eyes and his skin had taken on a pale blue pallor. Hadrian forsake any semblance of dignity and wept openly. No greater mourning had ever befallen an emperor. No greater mourning had befallen any human. Deep, guttural sounds of grief so vast and all-encompassing it nearly sucked his breath from him and robbed him of his own life. Hadrian railed against the profoundly denigrating emotions overtaking him. He turned to vomit. He soiled himself in the turmoil of this greatest of loss. He cared not. He uttered great, vehement curses. At the Nile. At the wine. At his own arms for not being strong enough to hold Antinous during the night. He took a deep, long breath and screamed into the brightening day. He reached for his blade, still tucked into its sheathe at his waist. Though he wore only a loincloth, it was rare that Caesar was ever unarmed. He pulled out the dagger and aimed it at his chest. "I shall not live without you, Antinous."

A bystander — an Egyptian — lunged at Hadrian and stayed his hand. "No, Caesar. You must not!" *Osiris, himself, divine god of the Nile flood, has spoken to my heart and I know Antinous shall achieve so much more than he could on this Earth. He is a god. He is part of Osiris now.* "I am a priest of Osiris, Caesar. I have heard the words of my god, most noble Emperor Pharoah."

Hadrian dropped his blade. "I cannot continue without him. Do you understand a love so deep that one heart is shared by two?" He hung his head and sighed. "If he is not to live at my side, then whatever divinity there is in me must pass to him. Antinous was more than a man to me. More precious than all the grains of sand in Egypt." Hadrian paused, carefully choosing his words. "I proclaim Antinous a god." He looked through swollen eyes at those gathered around him on the west bank of the river. He took note of the plaintive look on the face of the priest of Osiris hovering nearby. Hadrian, still holding his knife, opened his palm and slit a long gash from little finger to thumb. "By this blood, and by my divine right, I proclaim Antinous shall be remembered, as a man, and as he ascends into the afterlife, as a god. Let every man know his name. Let every man make offerings and sing praises. May his name be carved into stone to last ten thousand years and may all know he sits with Osiris in the afterlife. He shall be a benevolent god. A god of healing and beauty, for none were more pleasing to the eye than he." He placed his bloodied palm against Antinous' sallow chest, leaving a deep red imprint. "Hail Antinous, my lover. My god."

The crowd, once hushed, took this as their cue to respond to Hadrian's grief. The moments were shocking and horrific. Many drowned in the Nile. None were loved by the ruler of the known world. "Hail Antinous! Hail!" It was almost in unison—this sudden and fearfully coerced deification. There could be no other reply to Hadrian's tearful proclamation. To protest or laugh or show scorn or disdain would mean death. They knew it. And thus began their veneration of Antinous.

The Egyptian placed a hand on Hadrian's shoulder.

"Caesar." His voice soothed Hadrian.

"You are a priest of Osiris."

"Yes, mighty emperor…our god has spoken to us and has accepted Antinous into his arms. Hail the divine one, Osiris-Antinous. To drown in the Nile during the flood is most auspicious. Though Antinous may have fallen, or been pushed and murdered, or made the ultimate sacrifice—he now stands with Osiris. May he be remembered. Hail Antinous."

Hadrian took the man's hand. "Yes. Yes."

"Osiris accepts sacrifices during the inundation of the Nile. With our greatest sorrow at your loss and greatest rejoicing that it is this beautiful boy who now stands as divine with our god, let us celebrate his ascension."

"This is sacred ground. And here Antinous shall be honored. I shall build a city in this place with a great temple to Osiris and Antinous. I wish his tomb to rival the pyramids."

"We shall implore our builders to make it so," the priest replied.

"It shall be called Antinoöpolis." He wrapped Antinous' body even tighter in his arms. "He must be exalted. Remembered." He looked at the faces of the gathering crowd. "You, centurion!"

An older man in full armor stepped forward. "Caesar."

"Take Antinous' body and prepare it for burial. Not as a Roman, but as an Egyptian. Find an embalmer. Priest, do you know of a man dedicated to Osiris who can preserve Antinous' body?"

"Yes, Caesar. I shall lead your man to him, but please, the body must be moved from the water's edge and mud. It shall be cleaned and perfumed with great care prior to entering the preservation room. The entire process will take about forty-five days. Time enough to begin your city."

Hadrian released his grip on Antinous and allowed the centurion to lift Antinous from the mud and reeds. "Farewell, my love."

CHAPTER FIFTEEN

Adrian nearly toppled from the jolt of leaving the past behind. "I understand."

Antinous held his hand and helped keep him steady. "Yes. I bet you do."

"The only thing I can think of is a line from an Edgar Allen Poe poem. *We loved with a love that is more than love.*"

"Can you embrace the past and pull forward into our future?"

Adrian nodded. *Fuck.* "I think so. Yes. Let's get today's tours finished and we'll talk."

"With my death so fresh in your heart and mind, can we recreate the scene for your tourists?"

"Let's. I believe nothing in my life prepared me for this moment and yet I recall every second of your death and my grief in vivid detail." Adrian paused. He took a deep breath, then exhaled forcefully. "I am Hadrian."

CHAPTER SIXTEEN

drian accepted that he was in shock. His body was numb, and though he went through the motions of the passion play of Antinous' death, it was almost too real for his guests. He saw the looks on their faces.

Antinous took the reenactment very seriously. He laid along the shore, nude. Adrian had dressed in the *subligaria* and a simple tunic. He hoped the moral police of Egypt's far right did not arrest them. *He is a god, doing a god's work. Surely...no one will notice.*

He addressed his tour. "Due to a theft at the museum, traffic is backed up for hours in Cairo. The actors cannot join the afternoon tour. However, I, and our guest, Alexander, are very familiar with the event, and will perform for you. We hope it is as moving for you as it must have been for the original spectators. I hope you can appreciate our performance."

He crawled off the muddy bank and into the shallows where Antinous lay. He knelt and slipped his left arm around Antinous' back and his right across his chest. It wasn't hard to muster tears. The anguish of Hadrian still coursed through him. The raw pain of his lover's death was so fresh he felt it in every pore. The words he spoke weren't important…not really. He just spoke. He wept. He wept so hard he could not catch his breath, and at last, he said the words that proclaimed Antinous divine. *Has it been enough? Have I fulfilled the tour's performance without the troupe, or am I making six refunds?*

The faces of his guests gave him all the information he needed. When he looked up, after performing one of the greatest cathartic moments in Roman history, a few tissues were being passed between them. And then came the applause.

Antinous opened his eyes and smiled at Adrian. "You did it."

"We did it. Let's get you cleaned up before we are arrested for indecency."

Antinous rose and then unashamedly walked, caked in mud and dripping wet, toward Adrian's van. Adrian stood and shook off a swoon. He exhaled forcefully. Clearly, Antinous was beautiful. *Is beautiful.* He could not avert his gaze from the taunt body sauntering away from the Nile's edge. *And I can have that. Do I want that?* Adrian chuckled. *Oh, yes. I want that.*

As Adrian moved away from the mud, the applause continued. "Thank you. I'll clean up now and we can continue the tour."

The tour van was equipped with a small solar shower. A cubie of water on the roof, heated by the ever-present Egyptian sun, trickled through hoses until it sprinkled down on whomever chose to stand under the spout. A folding screen offered a modicum of privacy.

"I've never had to use this for myself after I got an apartment. I kept it in case we needed to cool down a tourist. This place...is hot," Adrian said, flipping the toggle switch to "on" for the water to begin its courses. He stripped out of his now drying muddy clothes and took a quick rinse. Antinous followed him under the shower.

"I enjoy the sight of your nakedness, Adrian. You are beautiful."

Adrian felt himself flush from ears to toes. "Thank you." *Thank you? How should I respond?* "Yes. I like how you look, too, incidentally." Adrian couldn't pull his gaze from the taught muscles of Antinous' body. "You have scars."

"From many a turn in the hills with bow and spear. I was not in battle."

Adrian slid his hand over Antinous' shoulder. "I'd like to kiss you."

"I am yours."

The tour guide and reincarnation of Hadrian gently pressed his lips against Antinous' mouth. A simple kiss — which opened the flood gates.

The only thing that mattered was Antinous' body next to his. Slick, sun-heated warmth of bronzed skin next to his tanned-only-in-places-that-saw-daylight, ushering arousal, and deep, penetrating memories mixing into glorious future.

Without any sense of decorum, they walked

from the shower into the van and then into the very back bench seat. All the windows were tinted, and the vehicle was far cooler than outside.

Adrian pulled out his spare clothes and then passed Antinous a white caftan.

"Should we dress, Adrian? Let us kiss nude and explore each other."

"The tour."

"They are occupied and thoroughly entertained."

Adrian slipped a crisp red tunic over his head. "We shouldn't."

"I will explode if I do not feel you in my arms this minute."

Adrian lowered his head and nodded. "I understand."

"Then come to me, my love."

*

Adrian leaned into Antinous, and they kissed. Deeply kissed. An exploratory kiss. States of full arousal blossomed. Antinous slid off the bench seat and kneeled before Adrian, then took an engorged member into his mouth. He had not fellated his love for nearly two thousand years. The penis felt the same as ever it had. The body odor was the same. The flavor—the same.

*

He didn't think he could relax. At any moment, someone could enter. He found that fact more exhilarating than problematic. The rhythm of Antinous' mouth and tongue against his dick…incredible. It had been a very long time since he'd taken a lover and he brimmed forthwith. Adrian moaned and grabbed Antinous' head of curls as he came, while Antinous sucked him dry.

Antinous pulled away and wiped his mouth with the back of his hand. "All hail Hadrian, emperor, beloved of Osiris, lover of Antinous and his reincarnation, Adrian, tour guide."

Adrian laughed. "Do you always give praise after fellatio?"

"Oh, yes. I would praise Hadrian while he fucked me and again when I sucked his cock. Of course when he fellated me, I became rapturous."

"Rapturous?"

"Completely ascendant."

"Did you ever fuck Hadrian?"

Antinous shook his head. "I am not Roman, therefore, I could not take a superior position. As his Greek lover, my body was under his. Often."

"Those laws do not apply today." Adrian looked sharply at Antinous and spoke with a low and sultry voice. "You shall have my ass."

"Thank you, Adrian."

"But now, let's get to the tour. I am eternally grateful that this van has all the accoutrements of home. I lived in this thing before I started making a little money doing the tours. Not only is there clothing stashed away, but dry goods and cooking implements."

"The shower is remarkable. Not unlike what Hadrian and I used—except we had servants pouring sun-heated water over us."

They finished dressing. The driver was at the far end of the bus, taking a smoke break. "Your group is just up a bit, looking at the ruins. I've been keeping my eye on the scammers. If any one of them gets too close, I'll take care of things. You…are busy, no?"

"Thanks, Mac."

"See you've found yourself a new friend. It's about time."

"I've been cautiously celibate for years."

Mac chuckled. "No longer."

"You saw?" Adrian asked, concerned.

"I heard. Can't see in the van what with those window films."

Adrian continued, "Have we breeched some rule of etiquette?"

"This is the desert, son. Rules don't apply once this far out. And I don't see any of Cairo's morality police about."

Adrian tugged on Antinous' arm, and they wandered to the group. The vendors had descended on his guests. It wasn't as bad as at the pyramids, when a tourist could get played if not in a tour group.

"You look very handsome in your Egyptian garb. The passion play was spectacular." Adrian couldn't remember the tourist's name. She was a devotee of Antinous—he knew that much.

"Thank you. We certainly played the parts today. Good thing we were able to get cleaned up."

"Adrian, when you wept as Hadrian must have wept with your friend here—who I must say is a spitting image for those we have of Antinous—my heart broke." She paused and held out her hand to

Antinous. "I'm Maggie. I'm an expat from the USA. I live full time in Jordan but came here for…*well*…your day."

Antinous shook her hand by embracing her forearm—the Roman way. "I am actually named Antinous. Very nice to meet you."

"You are a spitting image of the statues and portraits."

"I've been told that before."

"Well, I truly enjoyed your performance. Thank you, again."

Maggie wandered away, leaving Adrian and Antinous to their own devices.

"You know, Adrian, where I died and you wept is very close to the actual event."

"After all this time, you can still discern the location?"

"It glows. None of this was here. These ruins came after my death for the most part, but the place where I died, glows."

"Want to purchase a commemorative item celebrating your death and deification?"

Antinous laughed. "I do not but thank you for the offer."

Adrian squeezed his hand. "I'm going to mingle with the paying guests. Chat later?"

"I'm never leaving you again."

CHAPTER SEVENTEEN

Adrian took a deep breath and shook off the pleasure and giddiness of a new relationship—the rekindling of a very old relationship. *What the hell am I doing? What the hell is real?* He recalled the force of his recent orgasm. *That was real. Very real. Holy shit.* He put on his game face. Future tours depended upon good Yelp reviews. *What is my life now? I am the lover of an incredibly handsome young man, who is a god. A god. I am consort of a god. I can't do this...*

The vendors were out in full force, hawking Antinous-related trinkets in three languages. Some of them even took Venmo. Adrian picked up a pomegranate from a salesman, selling offerings. Salt, bay, rosemary sprigs, fruit. He cut it open at the stall before he carried it to the water's edge. Others had purchased balsawood sailboats and had sent them down river with a small candle or other item. Some had rolled up scraps of paper. Prayers. Wishes. Requests. *I made no wish. I barely offer prayers. And yet I am now aware of a very potent past life and reunited with his true love. My true love.*

He looked around and nodded to each member of his tour group in turn. Some were heavily laden with trinkets. "We need to leave for the pyramids shortly. Gather yourself and head back to the van."

"Hell of a tour, Adrian. Great job."

"Thank you. It's been one for the books, that's for sure. The driver will set out the picnic — but you might want to eat it inside the van to escape this heat."

The tourist laughed. "It's Egypt. What's a hundred degrees between friends?"

"Air conditioning is my friend. I used to live in that minibus."

"That's why you have the microwave and shower set up, huh?"

"Yes. My flat is much more comfortable."

"That kid…the one who everyone says looks like the statues…he one of the actors?"

Adrian pursed his lips and took a breath. *How do I answer this?* "He's so much more."

"Ah, is he one of the true believers?"

Adrian nodded. "Definitely."

* * * *

Antinous had not moved too far from the water's edge. The contrasts of desert and green fields were the same as it had always been. Beautiful. He watched Adrian move about the vendors and tourists with great ease. *Just like Hadrian. Comfortable with the people. I am his once again. My joy knows no bounds. I am his lover…and his god.*

He realized his skin was clammy and his steps grew heavy. He ignored the niggling feeling that something was amiss. The hairs on the back of his neck stood erect. The air had electrified, and it seemed a current coursed through him unbidden. It was uncomfortable but bearable. He scanned the Nile's edge. *I know this place. There were no roads save for caravan tracks. The encampment covered a great swath of desert, and we lived a good life here. Under these sands, I'm sure artifacts of that time remain. Buttons. Silver rings. Pottery. So many items of everyday life were used in this place. The mallet I wielded when I killed Marcus' woman. Is that here with her aggrieved spirit? Why do I consider her now? It's been nearly two thousand years. Is it her rage that penetrates my flesh, making it crawl as if scarabs cover me?* Antinous sucked in air, shallow and hard. This was not a divine presence of spirit. This was more akin to the sufferings and pains of mortality. His gut rolled and his skin burned. His vision blurred and his mouth went as dry as the sands upon which he stood. He heard screams and impact blows…then mewling whimpers.

A fleeting vision of his reincarnation agent flashed before him. *It is all falling apart.* Sharp, biting pains ripped at his internal organs. *I am imploding. No!* He closed his eyes as a stab sent him to his knees. He regained himself and found he was no longer in the Egypt of his reincarnation but was trapped in a shadow of a bygone era. Neither living, nor dead—a literal ghost of his past. Before him, Roman soldiers drank, drilled, polished their short swords, groomed horses, and fucked whores eager to earn a few coins to lift them from poverty. Except for Caesar's executioner. His hand was filled with a bloodied mallet and his gaze was fixed on the next spot in which to inflict damage. Antinous saw the lifeforce draining from the convicted like the gentle tendrils of a vine growing from rich soil, now desecrated and tainted with mold and urine. It rose from the top of the newly deceased's head, reaching higher and higher. It had an odor. Sweet, sickly. He knew the essence. It was indeed that of the whore he had killed to prove himself to Hadrian's men.

He winced and cried out with no one to hear him as long, jagged nails raked his cheeks. "Stop!" he cried.

"This is your reward for your years of service as the receptacle for Caesar's love. Nothingness."

"It is painful. Where is my reincarnation agent?"

"You were warned of fucking with the timeline. Did she not state that there could be consequences?"

Antinous vomited. Instead of hitting the sand, it became flames that pushed back against him. "She did."

"And because your lover proclaimed you divine in an excited utterance of grief, you believed you were above the conventions of time and space?"

He nodded. "I am a god. By Hadrian's words and Osiris' hands."

"Not so much now, Antinous. Not so much now."

"Osiris, help me."

"I died by your hand at the Nile's edge and the great gods of Egypt and Rome did not rally to my aid and raise me up. Why should any of them now heed your call? I have found no comfort these past two thousand years. I am a shade, walking in shadow, bleeding black blood from wounds that never heal. The last image of my life was your hand holding a mallet. I have hated you for far too long. I would see justice."

"I didn't know your name." His essence leaked from him. Every orifice. Eyes. Nose. Rectum. Urethra. What made him up, the waters of his life, now returned to the desert.

"And yet you struck me down and stood witness to my humiliation and crucifixion. I am not alone, you know. There are others cut by Caesar's orders that wander the banks of the Nile in search of light and drink and warmth. There are no resources for the departed of this dimension. We are trapped in a dry, barren land. Always do we observe life in its past glories and never can we interact or feel renewed by the coursing waters or heat of the sun. We are undead, Antinous. Our unfinished business keeps us prisoner, and now, because of your arrogance, you have joined us. I am the avenging angel of the timeline sent to return you to oblivion."

* * * *

Adrian doubled over as deep, rolling, searing pain overwhelmed him. He held his left side and dropped to his knees in the sand. The agony was exquisite. Not a damned person appeared to be coming to his aid. He saw the tourists and vendors and even a few soldiers in his periphery vision and no one seemed to notice he was nearly face-first in the sand, clutching his side. He took a breath, hoping it would clear his head and panicked as he observed Antinous disappear into a fog of flames and sand.

No. I must get to him. I cannot lose him again. He crawled to a toppled stone and pushed himself upright. The words stung his mind. *Lose. Him. Again.* As if he were now fully incorporated with the mystic DNA of Hadrian. For a second time. He placed one foot before the other. Antinous—or what was left of him—was not so far away that he could not crawl if he had to. The pain changed and crept away from his back left quadrant and settled into his legs. Like lifting lead weights, he stepped forward across the sand and mud until he lost his footing and fell before the blackened pile of ash where Antinous had once stood. *He is burnt to ash. There is nothing left.* As Hadrian had wept, so too did Adrian. He lifted handfuls of the blackened sand and clutched it to his chest. Tears fell freely and he made no attempt to stifle his anguish.

* * * *

From across the plains of existence between them, Antinous heard Adrian's cries. His heart sank and broke. He prostrated himself in agony.

*

The angry spirit stuck with him in the in between halted her torment. *What sweet misery this is that takes his attention from the suffering I bring. Why…I am nothing compared to it. What more can I do to him than have him witness the loss his lover feels? I did not expect to have my revenge so quickly. I anticipated a millennium of torment.*

Antinous sank deeper into despair and the bleakness of being utterly alone without hope. "Osiris, hear me. I cannot be without him. I cannot have him suffer so without me. We loved with a love that was more than love[1]. More than life. More than all the stars. What must I do?"

The answer came to him as if a cooling breeze had breached the boundaries of his dry death, and in that refreshing wind, he heard two simple words — *be humble.*

Antinous choked. *Humility? I am a god.* He assessed his situation, noting he was now very much alone. The vengeful whore had departed. *I am a trapped god, stuck between lives. I misused the timeline. I forsook conventions and insisted upon having my way when the threads of time are not lightly changed or pattern or woven in a pattern of my choosing.* "Osiris! I understand, but to show humility I must admit that my desire to be with Hadrian as we were is wrong. I did force my agent's hand and was not considerate of the timeline or lives changed by my actions, but I cannot display humility when my only goal is to hold him once

---

[1] Edgar Allen Poe, "Annabel Lee"

again. Hold him forever."

"You cannot go back." Osiris' voice sounded cold and tinny.

Antinous grit his teeth. "Give me the solution."

"You are divine."

"What can my divinity do to remedy this horrific situation?"

The blue-toned face of the god appeared as swirling mist. "Bring him here."

Antinous startled and bolted upright. "Bring him here? Bring him into this twilight land more barren and drier than any underworld?"

"Bring him *here*."

Antinous surveyed the movements and activities of the others living outside the veil. "Here? To Roman Egypt?"

"I will grant you freedom from any promises made to me and allow you and Hadrian to live in peace and die in each other's arms in old age. This place before you is made of memories and has no effect on the past or future. It simply is."

"Great Osiris, most generous of gods…"

"I cannot take his life. He must offer it."

"I do not believe Adrian would be amenable to suicide."

"Not suicide. If he bargains for your return as you did for Hadrian's…"

"I understand. He must offer all he has. All he is." Antinous sighed. "I don't know if his feelings are strong enough."

"We'll see."

CHAPTER EIGHTEEN

Adrian couldn't breathe. As if all life and breath were sucked from him, he struggled to keep every grain of sand in his hands. It was all he had left of Antinous. *Is this the result of the timeline issue he'd mentioned? What cruel trick is it that I only just come to grips with who I was, and what we could be…and he burns before my eyes and all that remains is charcoal and sand?* He closed his eyes. *Osiris, hear me. Although I have no right to call upon you, or any god, for I am not devout, nor even slightly religious, I must see him returned to me. Antinous. What passed between us and what will pass between us in the future…I cannot forsake it.* He wiped away tears, blackening his cheeks. "Teach me what I must do."

He gave no thought to his tour, the activity at the ruins, his van. As if moved by unseen hands, he rose and then walked solemnly to the edge of the

Nile. The pain with each step was unreal. The air burned him but he continued. "Osiris, here, along the banks of this most sacred river, during this fertile time of the inundation, I swear I will make an offering to you greater than any other. I *believe*. And that I offer. My belief. My devotion. What I am, is yours."

He held fast to the handfuls of sooty sand as new horrors coursed through his body. It started at his toes and flowed upward through his veins. Fiery, searing pain. He gripped the sand tighter and withheld the cry of anguish stuck in his throat. He swallowed fear, agony, hopelessness...his life as he descended into the Nile.

* * * *

Eons passed for Antinous. Ages of loneliness and angst. Around him the memories ebbed and flowed, but he remained unseen. Unheard. Cold. He even wished for the angry spirit of the woman he'd killed to appear to break the monotony. *This is the punishment for my arrogance. Adrian suffers and I, more so, for knowing it was I who caused his unhappiness.*

He curled into a fetal position on the sand. He could walk around...observe the living memories about him, stand at the Nile's edge and remember the feel of its coolness on a scorching day...but he could not interact. Truly, it was the cruelest death.

He closed his eyes. He was too dry for tears.

When he opened his eyes, he was in Hadrian's arms. In their tent. The sound of soldiers echoed through the fabric. He heard laughter. Antinous bolted upright. "What is this? Further punishment for my godly arrogance?"

"No. This is your reward. It is mine, as well."

The man looked like Hadrian. From the black curls to the taut muscles and well-worn sandals. "Are you he?"

"I am Adrian. At least a part of me is Adrian. I don't understand it, either. I am emperor and tour guide. First century Roman and twenty-first century expat. Antinous…we are reunited."

"This place is but memory."

"When you brought me to Roman Egypt, was that memory or time travel?"

Antinous touched Hadrian's chest. "It was both but neither. I used my divine prowess to join two timelines and bind you to your past."

"And my future."

"Osiris has forgiven my pridefulness." Antinous had not removed his hand from Hadrian's chest. He felt the warmth of the flesh. The sweat. The heat rising from pores and a heartbeat. There was a heartbeat. He raised Adrian's hand and kissed the scarred palm. "It is you."

"The great Osiris heard my prayers to be reunited with you. Perhaps this is the gentler scenario for the timeline. Adrian need not continue. His…my affairs…are in order. Truthfully, I am relieved I can embrace this…life." He pressed Antinous' hand to his chest with his own. "I know this world. I know Hadrian dies of old age safe in his bed, but in this world, you will be by my side. Of this I am certain. Our second chance lies in our shared past. We can make a future in this place."

Antinous laughed. "This is our past, but you are Hadrian and Adrian, and with each breath, we are propelled into the future. So very confusing is this timeline."

"I think the idea is not to think about it too hard. Just..." Adrian turned and waved his hand at the Nile. "Go with the flow."

"Where you go, go I."

Adrian pushed Antinous onto some pillows. "Put yourself to me. Inside me. I have waited nearly two thousand years and countless lifetimes to feel you deeply."

Antinous fumbled with Adrian's robes. "Hail Caesar."

The End

ABOUT THE AUTHOR

Darragha Foster is an award-winning paranormal romance author who finds inspiration in everyday life. Even in the cold case at the grocer—where she's no longer allowed. She also writes as JJ Andrews (Hexing Harlots series).

Find Darragha at:
darragha@darragha.com
TikTok: @darraghafoster
IG: @darragha
Facebook: Darragha Foster